"How much would it complicate things if I kissed you right now?"

Yes! Outwardly, she strove for a semblance of calm. She could control this, she could, she silently insisted. This was purely a physical thing, nothing more. "That all depends."

"On?" he prodded.

Just the slightest hint of a smile curved her lips. "On the way you kiss."

Very slowly and carefully, Jackson silently released the breath he'd been holding. "Are you game to find out?"

She lifted her chin. "I've never turned my back on a challenge."

"Good thing to know," he told her just before he slipped his arms around her and drew her closer to him. His mouth came down on hers.

Dear Reader,

Here we are with the second installment of MATCHMAKING MAMAS. This time it's soft-spoken Theresa Manetti who is trying to find a mate for her workaholic daughter. Kate has only ventured out into the dating field a handful of times. The last time was not the charm, inasmuch as she became engaged to a high-profile criminal lawyer who enjoyed more than his share of "undercover" work, the undercover in this case being sheets. After that disaster, Kate dedicated herself to building up her career and completely ignoring her personal life.

Until she meets district bank manager Jackson Wainwright. After building up a successful career, Jackson finds himself coming back to his roots because of his older brother, Jonah, a charming man with a seriously addictive personality. Assuming the role of his brother's keeper, Jackson finds himself in need of a family lawyer, which leads him to Kate. The rest is history.

I hope you enjoy this newest installment. From the bottom of my heart, I wish you someone to love who loves you back.

All the best,

Marie Ferrarella

FIXED UP WITH MR. RIGHT?

MARIE FERRARELLA

SPECIAL EDITION

Published by Silhouette Books

America's Publisher of Contemporary Romance

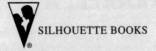 SILHOUETTE BOOKS

Recycling programs
for this product may
not exist in your area.

ISBN-13: 978-0-373-65523-6

FIXED UP WITH MR. RIGHT?

Printed in U.S.A.

Books by Marie Ferrarella

MARIE FERRARELLA

This *USA TODAY* bestselling and RITA® Award-winning author has written almost two hundred novels for Silhouette Books, some under the name Marie Nicole. Her romances are beloved by fans worldwide. Visit her Web site at www.marieferrarella.com.

To
Persis Choksy,
operations supervisor
at Wells Fargo,
for kindly answering all my questions

Chapter One

"You're kidding."

When her cell phone began to ring, Katherine Colleen Manetti, K. Manetti according to the silver scripted initials on her office door, had debated letting the call go to voice mail. She was almost too busy to breathe.

When she saw that the call was from Nikki Connors, one of her two oldest, dearest friends, she'd decided to give herself a quick, unscheduled break before she headed off to court. Talking to Nikki—or to Jewel Parnell, her other best friend—reminded her that there was a life outside of the prestigious family law firm where she seemed to spend most of her waking hours.

"Talk quick." Kate popped out a small mirror from

the middle drawer of her desk to make sure that every silken, shoulder-length, midnight black hair was in place. It saved her a trip to the ladies' room. "I've got to fly out of the office in less than five minutes."

"Kate, I don't have a date yet, but I need you to be my maid of honor. You and Jewel. You don't mind splitting the position with Jewel, do you? Because I really can't choose between you."

"Hold it. Why do you need a maid of honor?"

Kate knew the logical answer, but it just didn't fit. All three of them were too busy forging their careers to date, much less date long enough to create the need to utter vows before a saintly looking priest.

"Because I'm getting married."

Kate couldn't remember Nikki *ever* sounding this happy, not even when she graduated medical school near the top of her class. "Married?" she echoed in complete stunned disbelief. Light blue eyes narrowed as the twenty-nine-year-old attorney tried to wrap her head around the concept. "As in ''til death do us part'?"

It took Nikki a second to answer. Kate had strong suspicions that her friend was almost too happy to talk. What was *that* like? she wondered. She'd been engaged once a couple of years ago, but that had blown up in her face when Matthew McBain, the tall, dark and gorgeous criminal lawyer who'd taken custody of her heart turned out to be more interested in carving notches into his headboard then being faithful to her.

That was when she'd admitted that she had been

living the reverse of that old adage about kissing a lot of frogs to find a prince. In her case, she kissed a lot of princes only to discover that they were really frogs. And none had been a bigger frog than Matthew. That was when she'd decided to give her career center stage in her life. Careers, at least, gave back what you put into them. They didn't sleep around.

"Yes," Nikki assured her. "That kind of married."

"To a man?"

"Yes," Nikki said, laughing.

And then Kate remembered. At their last quickie get-together, Nikki had mentioned that she was seeing someone. To be honest, she hadn't paid all that much attention. But she was paying attention now.

"The guy with the kid?" Kate recalled.

"Yes, the guy with the kid." She could *hear* the smile in Nikki's voice. "I'm getting two for the price of one."

That was when Kate had blurted out, "You're kidding." The next moment, she remembered the way Nikki had met this supposed Prince Charming and his offspring. "The one your mother set you up with?" There was barely veiled horror in Kate's voice, not to mention apprehension.

"Technically, my mother didn't actually set me up with him, Kate. She sold Lucas a house and, because he was new to the area, he asked if she knew the name of a good pediatrician. She gave him my name *only* because he asked."

That wasn't the way Kate saw it.

"Po-tay-to, po-tah-to. It was a setup, Nik. You know it was a setup. *I* know it was a setup. And you know what else?"

"What else, Kate?"

"Now that your mother's had this success, that just empowers the rest of them to go crazy and *really* meddle in our lives—mine and Jewel's," she clarified. "Oh God, Nik, can't you just live with him in sin? Do it for Jewel and me. Otherwise, we're doomed."

"Kate, it's not that bad," Nikki assured her, amused.

"Did all that happiness I hear in your voice give you amnesia? Don't you remember what it was like when we were in college, constantly dodging all those men our mothers kept throwing in our path?" Kate shivered, remembering. "You know what they're like. A tiny taste of success keeps them going for months. I'd be surprised if there isn't some guy on my doorstep all wrapped up in a red ribbon by the time I get home tonight."

"Are you through?"

Kate sighed. "For now."

"Okay. Back to the reason I called. Can I count on you to stand up for me?"

Resigned, Kate said, "Yes, you can count on me to stand up for you. But make the wedding soon, okay? I'm going to have to get out of town, at least until this blows over. There'll be no living with my mother after this."

"You don't live with your mother," Nikki pointed out. "You hardly see your mother."

"There's a reason for that." It wasn't that she didn't

love her mother, she did. A great deal. And in order for that love to continue, there needed to be space between them. At times *lots* of space. "Mom's old-fashioned. She doesn't think a woman's complete without a man." There was a knock on her door and then it opened. Her brother, Kullen, stuck his head in. "Or that a man's complete without a woman, for that matter," she added.

Coming in, Kullen took hold of her wrist and turned it so that he could see who she was on the phone with. He recognized Nikki's number. "Very true," he agreed. "And the more women he has, the more complete that man is." He grinned broadly. Unlike his sister, he had a very full social life. Their mother would have argued that it was *too* full. Kullen never allowed himself to linger with anyone long enough to even remotely become serious. "C'mon, Kate, it's getting late. We've gotta go," he urged.

On the other end of the call, Nikki said, "Me, too. Say hi to Kullen for me," she requested cheerfully.

"Right. I'll talk to you later, Nik." After terminating the call, Kate tucked the cell phone into her pocket. As she rose to her feet, she saw the unspoken question in her older brother's eyes. "Nikki's getting married."

Kullen's mouth dropped open. "You're kidding."

"That was my reaction, too," Kate told him, "and no, I'm not."

Kullen held the door open for her. He and his sister were both heading for the courthouse on Jamboree. His sports car was in the shop—again—and he was getting a ride from Kate who admittedly drove a far more reliable car than his. But his was by far the more attractive one.

Reaching the elevator first, Kullen pressed the down button. "So who's the lucky guy?"

God, this was going to be awful, Kate thought. She could feel it in her bones. She'd just begun enjoying the fact that her mother had stopped trying to work her dating life—or lack thereof—into every conversation they had.

"Some guy that her mother set her up with."

Kullen looked surprised. "I thought Nikki was against that kind of thing."

"She is. Her mother was underhanded about it." Kate frowned. "You know what this means, don't you?"

Amusement highlighted Kullen's face. "We start screening our calls?"

"Not funny, Kullen. In the past year Mom's finally slacked off. What this means is that she's going to go back to her old ways."

The elevator arrived. Getting on, they had the elevator to themselves for once. Kullen laughed. "You make it sound like a war."

Kate tossed her head. Jet-black hair strained against an army of pins. She always wore it up when she went to court. "That's because that's exactly what it is."

And they both knew it.

"I have to hand it to you, Maizie." Admiration fairly vibrated in Theresa Manetti's voice. "When you first started pushing this idea of using our businesses as a starting point for finding husbands for our girls, I really had my doubts."

Theresa looked at the woman she had known since the third grade. There were cards in her hand, but the weekly poker game she, Maizie and Cecilia were supposedly engaged in wasn't remotely holding her attention. Maizie had just announced that her daughter, Nikki, was engaged. Maizie had done it. She'd found a suitable man for her daughter just as she'd set out to do. It was a goal they all aspired to.

"But you did it," Theresa declared with unabashed admiration. "You found a man for Nikki *and* the two of you are still on speaking terms. That's quite a feat in my book. Can you find one of those for me?" When she saw Cecilia looking at her with a puzzled expression, Theresa realized she hadn't made herself clear. "I mean find a man for Kate." With a sigh, she said for the umpteenth time what they all knew was true. "Ever since that horrid Matthew made mincemeat out of her heart, she keeps saying she has no intentions of getting married. That her career is enough for her."

Maizie listened with a sympathetic ear. "What she needs is a good man to make her reassess her stand." There was unwavering confidence in her eyes as she assured her friend, "Between the three of us, we'll find someone."

"The three of us?" Cecilia repeated. There was a skeptical note in her voice.

This was never meant to be a solo operation. Maizie firmly believed that there was strength in numbers.

"Sure. I sell houses, you have a cleaning service that goes into some of the best residential homes in Orange County and *you*—" Maizie shifted her sharp blue eyes in Theresa's direction "—cater affairs. We come in close contact with a lot more people than the average person. I *know* we can find two decent men in that pool."

It wasn't that Theresa didn't want to help, it was just that she knew her weaknesses as well as her strengths. Her strengths were love and cooking. Under weaknesses she could list social relationships. "You're so much better than I am at this sort of thing," Theresa told her friends.

"Don't sell yourself short, Theresa. You are probably the sweetest person I know." She glanced at Cecilia. "No offense, Cecilia."

Cecilia looked completely unfazed. "None taken," she assured Maizie. "Everyone knows what a sweetheart Theresa is."

"Don't worry, Theresa. We have three times the playing field, three times the possibilities. Just stay alert and who knows?" She winked. "This time next year, we might all be shopping for baby clothes."

"From your mouth to God's ear," Theresa murmured.

"Exactly," Maizie agreed with a huge, amused grin.

Maizie's words were still ringing in her ears the next day when Theresa made her way into Republic National Bank's corporate office to meet with Jackson Wainwright, a prospective client. When a very efficient assistant brought her in to meet with the man who required her services, those words were replaced by two: breath-takingly gorgeous.

If Theresa could have drawn a picture of the man she knew would make her daughter sit up and take notice, this was the man she would have drawn.

Tall, almost incredibly handsome, Jackson Wainwright brought the word *dashing* to mind. Granted it was an old-fashioned description, but looking at the raven-haired man with his chiseled profile, his magnetic blue eyes and his broad shoulders brought the heroes she'd grown up watching and worshipping on the silver screen to mind.

At the moment, the man was on the phone—and not happily so. Nodding a silent greeting, he tried to wrap up the call as he gestured for her to sit down in the chair before his desk.

It was obvious that the person on the other end of the line was a source of irritation to him, even though he kept his voice low.

"I don't have time to argue with you, Jonah. The answer is no, I'm not going to lend you any more money. You need money, come in and we'll see about getting you a job."

Theresa watched as he pressed his lips together and replaced the receiver without another word. The man on the other end of the line had obviously hung up.

The apologetic smile her client-to-be flashed her instantly lit up the room. "I'm sorry."

"There's no reason to apologize, Mr. Wainwright.

I'm the one who walked in on you." She knew she should just let the matter drop, but she wouldn't have been Theresa if she hadn't asked, "Family trouble?"

The fact that the woman asked—and guessed correctly—took him aback. Strained, his guard momentarily down, he heard himself asking, "How can you tell?"

Theresa nodded at his right hand. "Your knuckles turned white on the receiver." And then she smiled understandingly. "I've found that family can get to us the way no one else can. I love my two children more than life itself, but there are times I could strangle them."

Jackson wasn't secretive by nature, but neither did he bare his soul to the first stranger he encountered. Yet there was something warm and understanding about this woman—and he was on overload. A great deal of that was because of Jonah.

He'd expressly taken this transfer from San Francisco back to his old hometown because it was impossible to keep tabs on Jonah from over four hundred miles away. Lately, Jonah seemed even keener than usual to head down a path of self-destruction. He'd been in town less than a week and he was already at odds with his older brother. It had gotten to the point where it was a case of either talking about it, or exploding.

Jackson talked.

"I can certainly relate to that," he told the woman with the sweet, heart-shaped face. "My brother Jonah is a big, overgrown kid who just never grew up."

"Younger brother?" she guessed.

"Older," he told her, shaking his head. "That's the funny part. Jonah was supposed to be the wiser one."

"Not necessarily," she said kindly. "A person's temperament, not the order of his birth, has a great deal to do with the way he—or she—reacts to responsibility."

About to comment, Jackson stopped himself. "I'm sorry, I didn't ask you to come here to listen to me complain."

Theresa smiled at him. "That's one of the fringe benefits of doing business with Theresa's Catering. I'm Theresa." She leaned forward, extending her hand to him.

Jackson felt himself responding to the woman's guileless warmth immediately. "I'm very pleased to meet you, Theresa."

He had a good, strong handshake, Theresa noted. Her father had always maintained that you could tell a lot about a man by his handshake. Jackson's said he was a man who was not afraid to take charge and who had the courage of his convictions. She liked that.

"Have you been your brother's keeper for long?" she asked with sincere interest.

The question made him laugh. He hadn't thought of himself in those terms, but this soft-voiced woman had hit the nail right on the head.

"Ever since my parents died," he told her. Right now, it felt like an eternity ago.

This transfer that he had initiated came with its own baggage, which only added to the weight pressing down on his shoulders. On top of that, the family lawyer,

Morton Bloom, the official juggler of all the balls, hadn't woken up last Monday morning. Seemingly healthy and robust, the sixty-eight-year-old man had died in his sleep. He had no partners, no one to step into his shoes.

This just when he'd made up his mind to have Mort change the way Jonah's trust fund had been worded.

Feeling vulnerable and strangely connected to this woman who was so easy to talk to, Jackson, half kidding, asked, "You wouldn't happen to know the name of a good lawyer, would you?"

He hadn't really expected an answer, but he got one. "I know several, Mr. Wainwright. What kind of a lawyer are you looking for?"

"A patient one." Instantly, he flashed that smile Theresa was fairly certain Kate would find bone-melting. She knew that if she was twenty-nine years young, she would have. "Sorry," he apologized for the second time in five minutes, "that was flippant, although the lawyer I need would *have* to be patient because part of his job would be to deal with my brother. I need a family lawyer," he specified. Jackson sighed. "It's been a rough few days, Mrs. Manetti. Now, about the party—"

As a rule, Theresa never interrupted a client. But this could be the only opening that would allow her to introduce Jackson to her daughter. So she broke her own rule and cut in. "I know two excellent family lawyers."

Jackson stopped, surprised. And then he shrugged. What did he have to lose? "Why don't you give me their names when we finish?"

Theresa had a better idea. "Why don't I give them to you now and get that out of the way?" she countered. "Then we're free to concentrate on the details of the party."

"All right," he said agreeably. "Give me their names and numbers."

Theresa wrote both names down, and just this once, she decided to go along with Kate's initial insistence on using her initials to hide her gender in an attempt to gain a foothold in what still was a male-dominated world.

Jackson took the paper from her when she finished writing. The neat, careful lettering impressed him. You didn't see handwriting like that anymore, he thought. And then he noted the names. *K. C. Manetti and Kullen Manetti.*

"Manetti?" he repeated. Amused, he asked, "Any relation?"

Theresa returned his smile. "Those children I sometimes want to strangle?" she said, recalling her initial reference. "Those are their names. They also happen to be excellent lawyers," she said proudly, adding, "They take after their late father."

"I'll give them a call," he told her, pocketing the paper.

Theresa drew in a deep breath, mentally crossing her fingers. She'd done all she could—for now. "Why don't you tell me what you had in mind."

Jackson blinked. "Excuse me?"

"For the party," Theresa prompted.

"Right. Sorry." What was that, his third apology to

this woman? Yet somehow, he felt that she understood. Her eyes were sympathetic. "I'm just a bit on overload right now."

"If this is a bad time," Theresa began.

She was perfectly willing to postpone any further discussion until it was more convenient for Jackson. As far as she was concerned, she'd already accomplished far more than she ever thought she could. The sooner she left, the sooner she would be able to drive to St Anne's and light a few candles. Never hurt to have backup.

"Between you and me, Mrs. Manetti, I've got a feeling that there's not going to be a better time," Jackson confided. "At least not for a while." He settled back at his desk. "Let me tell you what I had in mind...."

There was a quick rap on Kate's door and then Kullen poked his head in. "Hey, Kate, I need a favor."

Impatient because she was trying to finish something, Kate spared him a fleeting look.

"I'm not going to call another one of your five-night stands and tell her you've been called out of town. You want to break up with somebody? You're a big boy, you can do it yourself."

"First of all, she's not a five-night stand. I've been seeing Allison for two weeks now—"

"Alert the media," Kate deadpanned.

He pretended not to hear. "And two, it's nothing like that. I didn't realize that I'm due in Tustin in half an hour. Sheila accidentally scheduled a new client to come in at twelve-thirty. Do me a favor and take him for me."

She stopped typing and leaned back in her chair to look at her brother. He sounded entirely too innocent. "What's the catch?"

Kullen spread his hands wide, giving her his best innocent look. "No catch. Jackson Wainwright's a new client. His family lawyer suddenly died on him just as Wainwright needed to have some business straightened out. I gather it has to do with a trust fund." Kullen cocked his head as he looked at Kate. "You're up to that, aren't you?" He knew that nothing got his sister going faster than a challenge to her abilities. "Just start the ball rolling for me. We've got the same last name. He'll think you're me."

"Only if the man's legally blind," she pointed out.

"I am the prettier one," Kullen agreed, then ducked, laughing, as Kate threw a crumpled sheet of paper at him. She missed hitting him by a good two feet. "You throw like a girl," he crowed.

"There's a reason for that." Kate glanced at her desk calendar. "I can give this Wainwright guy half an hour, no more. After that, I've got to go to the courthouse to file Mrs. Greenfield's name change."

Kullen glanced at his watch. "Gotta run."

"You owe me one," Kate called after his retreating back.

"I'm good for it." Kullen smiled to himself as he made his way down the hall.

* * *

Kate was so immersed in what she was doing, she didn't hear the knock on her door until it came again, a little louder this time. Kate blew out a breath. *Now what?*

Her life was measured out in fifteen-minute increments. It was twelve-twenty. She had ten more minutes before Kullen's new client showed up.

"Come in, Sheila," she called out without bothering to look up. Not wanting to lose her place, she continued typing. "I'll be with you in a minute. I just need to finish this before my brother's castoff comes in." Kate heard the door open and close. "Whatever you're bringing, just drop it on my desk." She typed in the final line. "There, done!" she declared triumphantly.

Looking up, Kate was startled to see an incredibly handsome man in a custom tailored suit. Moreover, he was sitting in front of her desk, smiling at her. How— and when—had that happened?

"Hello," she said a little uncertainly.

"Hi."

When he didn't say anything else, she asked, "And you are?"

The smile on his lips deepened just a touch. "Your brother's castoff, I believe."

Oh God, why hadn't she looked up when she heard the knock? And what was Sheila doing, allowing clients to wander around by themselves? The woman was practically a fixture in the office ever since her father had hired her, but that was no excuse to let a client just walk in.

"Jackson Wainwright?" she guessed.

The man inclined his head. "The very same."

Damage control. She cleared her throat. "Of course I meant castoff in the best possible sense of the word."

There was a hint of amusement in his eyes. "I didn't realize that there *was* a best possible sense of the word regarding castoffs."

"I'm so sorry, I—" Kate could feel the rush of color coming up to her cheeks. Blushing was one of the things her father used to upbraid her for, telling her she'd never make a good lawyer as long as she had that flaw. She'd thought that she'd conquered it.

Obviously she was having a relapse.

Kate rose to her feet. "Excuse me," she said to Jackson as she passed him, striding out of her office. From the corner of her eye, she saw that her brother's twelve-thirty appointment rose to his feet. To leave, as well?

But when she opened the door again a beat later, Jackson Wainwright was still standing right where she'd left him, looking somewhat bewildered as he stared at the door.

With a purposeful, confident stride, Kate reentered the office, walked up to Kullen's client and extended her hand to him. "Hello, I'm Katherine Manetti." She saw the uncertain expression on the man's handsome face deepen. She could almost guess what he was thinking. Smiling serenely—she said, "This is called, 'first impression, take two.'"

For a moment, she thought he was going to walk out.

The sound of Jackson Wainwright's deep, resonant laughter told Kate that he'd decided to stay. Which meant she'd just gotten that second chance she was after.

Kate released the breath she hadn't realized until now that she'd been holding.

Chapter Two

Sitting up a little straighter in her chair, Kate discreetly took another breath, smiled and asked, "So, what is it that can I do for you, Mr. Wainwright?"

Several things came to mind, entirely unbidden, surprising him as much as they would have her, if he'd said them aloud. Luckily, he'd learned long ago to keep his own counsel and hold his tongue. But just for the moment, because the last two weeks had been unbelievably hectic and stressful, what with tying up all the loose ends where he'd worked, packing up all his belongings and dealing with his brother far more than he was accustomed to, Jackson allowed himself a single quick flight of fancy.

It coaxed an entirely different sort of smile from his lips.

His audience of one caught her breath again. This had to be the most seductive, sexy smile she had seen in a very long time. Lucky thing that she was immune to sexy. She had Matthew to thank for that. Matthew and the string of good-looking, soulless men who'd come before him.

A full five seconds of silence lapsed before Jackson finally spoke. "I'm new in town." Realizing that wasn't actually a true statement, he corrected himself. "Well, old-new."

"Excuse me?"

"I grew up in Bedford," he explained.

"But then you spread your wings and flew?"

He smiled again. "I flew."

His eyes crinkled when he smiled, she noted. The next moment, she upbraided herself for even noticing. But at least he didn't take themselves too seriously, and that was a good thing. "And how long has it been since you've 'flown'?"

Now that he was back, it seemed like only yesterday that he'd left home. But it wasn't. "A dozen years—if you count college."

"College counts," she affirmed. Because she saw no reason to curtail her curiosity and the information might prove useful to know down the line, she asked, "What brought you back?"

"A promotion—and family business," he finally said after a thoughtful pause.

"Which has the greater weight?" She kept her eyes on his, fairly certain that she would be able to tell if he was just paying lip service, or if he ultimately meant what he said. She'd become very good at spotting liars, also thanks to Matthew. Mining some good out of the experience was the only way she could forgive herself for being such a fool.

There was another pause on his part. And then he said, "I'm not sure yet."

Actually, Jackson thought, that was a lie. He knew damn well which of the two carried the greater weight for him. Knew, too, that he resented it for that reason. It had been drummed into his soul that family always came first. And if that wasn't enough, his mother's deathbed request was that he "look out for Jonah." Because he'd loved her, he'd promised.

And now, if not for his promise, he would have been content to spend the rest of his life living and working in the Bay area. San Francisco was an exciting city. There was always something going on, something to entertain a man, or to challenge him. The restaurants weren't too shabby, either. He considered himself a cosmopolitan kind of man and San Francisco suited his purposes just fine, thank you.

But despite the lure of the city, he couldn't very well turn his back on Jonah, especially since he was all Jonah had—whether Jonah acknowledged that little fact or not. Moreover, he was just possibly all that stood between Jonah and absolute self-destruction.

Kate nodded, digesting his answer. "At least you're honest."

He flashed a smile. "I have to be. It's written into my contract." The puzzled look returned to her eyes. Jackson elaborated. "I'm a district manager at Republic National Bank," he explained. "People like their bank executives honest."

She thought of the current economic climate. Kate had no doubt that it would continue in its present venue for a while to come. She was, at bottom—when the matter didn't involve romance—too optimistic a person to entertain the idea that it would ultimately collapse. This was what made her her mother's daughter rather than her father's. Anthony Manetti had been a born pessimist.

"These days," she replied, "they just like them to be solvent—and to refrain from recklessly spending the share holders' assets."

This time, the smile on his lips held no humor behind it. "Sadly, that's my brother's department. Which brings us back to why I'm here. Our longtime family lawyer, Morton Bloom, died somewhere in the night between last Sunday and Monday."

Kate realized that she was being "auditioned" for the position of his new family lawyer. She tried to look properly sympathetic. "I'm sorry to hear that."

What he heard in her voice—sincerity mixed with compassion—caught him off guard. He could think of only one explanation. "You knew him?"

"No." She'd never met the man. After that fiasco

with Matt—which included mistaking him for a decent human being—Kullen was the only lawyer she socialized with these days. "But you did. I imagine that when someone you've known for a long time dies, it does shake you up to a degree."

Until she said that, he wasn't sure how he felt one way or another about Mort's death, other than being annoyed because it was an inconvenience. Now, instead of coming down for the week to conduct his business with the lawyer, he had to move down here, watch out for Jonah and search for a new lawyer, all while familiarizing himself with an entirely new set of people and terrain in the district he was taking on.

He supposed his attitude toward Mort could be viewed as rather callous. He wasn't a callous person by nature. He liked to think of himself as compassionate. But anything that had to do with Jonah instantly had his back going up.

It was a far cry from when he was a boy and he'd idolized his brother. Sunny, gregarious, with a knack of making people forgive him, Jonah had been the center of everyone's universe—until he and his parents realized just how weak a character Jonah had.

Jackson could still remember accidentally coming across his mother sitting alone in the dark in her room, her fingers all but knotted together. She was softly crying to herself. It was the first time Jonah had been taken to the hospital. He'd been ten and Jonah had been fourteen. He'd thought his brother was sick. In a way, he supposed he'd been right. Drug addiction was a sickness and Jonah had overdosed.

That was when the crown that he had placed on his brother's head first began to slip. He'd always been fiercely protective of his mother and anything that hurt her instantly earned his fury. He remembered wanting to punch Jonah out despite the fact that his brother was twice his size.

"After a while you get used to it," he continued when he realized that too much silence had gone by. That had to sound cold and distant to the woman. He wasn't exactly sure why, but he wasn't comfortable with her thinking of him in that light. "My parents died in a car accident," he explained. "And there was a girl when I was in college…"

Jackson punctuated his sentence with a shrug. He wasn't about to go there right now. Wasn't about to revisit the way he'd felt when his college roommate had shaken him awake to tell him that Rachel had been struck by a drunk driver who'd lost his way and somehow had wound up on the campus. The man was going ninety on the twilight-darkened streets when he hit her. The driver wouldn't have stopped except that he wound up plowing his brand-new Ferrari into a tree. Rachel had been making her way through the crosswalk, on her way to her dorm when he ran her down. Both she and the drunken bastard were dead before the ambulance arrived.

Kate could almost literally feel the emotions vibrating around Wainwright. Was he telling her the truth, or was this something he was just saying for effect? From her experience, handsome men liked to cast themselves in a good light early on.

"I'm sorry," she said quietly.

"Thank you," Jackson answered stiffly. "But I'm here about the living." He thought of how reckless Jonah was becoming and what he'd gotten himself into this time. "Although I'm not sure just how much longer that's going to be true."

"You're going to have to explain that."

Yes, he supposed he should. "My brother has an addictive personality." All the signs had been there from the beginning, but no one wanted to admit it. "Every time he cleans up his act in one department, he latches onto something else, another crutch to help him stand upright—or reasonably so." Jackson paused to recall the correct order. "He has, by turns, been a drug addict, an alcoholic, a religious zealot, a food addict and—this is his latest craze—a gambling addict."

Being his brother had to be a heavy burden, Kate thought, suddenly very grateful that all Kullen did was collect lightweight girlfriends who had the IQ of a shoelace. "I'm sorry to hear that."

He laughed shortly. "If he didn't have an addictive personality, I wouldn't be here, so for you this might be a good thing."

That was rather a cynical remark, despite the fact that he punctuated it with a smile. "You do plan to explain that, too, right?"

Regarding her for a moment, Jackson made a decision. "I do, but not on an empty stomach. Do you have any plans for lunch?"

That caught her off guard. "Other than eating it, no. But I do have to file some papers at the courthouse this afternoon."

He had to get back to the office himself, but that wasn't for a couple of hours. Would she be leaving before then? "Is there a set time?"

Although she'd planned to get there in another half hour or so, in actuality she just had to get there before they closed for the day. "Before five."

He nodded. "Good. We'll be done with phase one by then."

The man definitely talked in riddles. "Phase one?"

"Getting to know each other."

A red light went off in her head. Was this a business meeting, or was it all a sham? Her eyes narrowed. "I'm afraid I don't follow."

"You won't be following. You'll be in my car. Parking will be easier that way." He was already rising to his feet.

Kate put up her hand like a traffic cop. "Wait, hold it," she ordered. He needed to clear this up for her. If he was a client, she'd cut him a little slack. But if he was trying to come on to her, there was no way she was going to go along with this. She didn't need another good-looking man creating havoc in her life. "Just why do we need to get to know each other?"

"Well, it doesn't have to be reciprocal if you choose not to ask any questions, but I for one need to get to know you." His eyes held hers as he made his point. "You don't expect me to just entrust the family fortune to you without knowing who I'm dealing with."

Maybe being in a crowded restaurant with this man wasn't such a bad idea. Although they were speaking mostly in generalities, there was this undercurrent of intimacy she found impossible to shake—or to understand. And when he looked at her like that, she caught herself thinking things that weren't entirely professional even though her guard was up.

"I'm assuming that you're here on someone's recommendation," she speculated. A recommendation should count for something with this man.

Sitting down again, Jackson smiled and she found that, just for a split second, she needed to remind herself to breathe. Alarms started going off in her head—but she couldn't very well just walk away from a client. The head of the firm, Harrison Rothchild, her father's successor, wasn't a very understanding or forgiving man.

"I am, actually," he told her, "but the recommendation was hardly unbiased."

She could see how that would happen. All of her clients as well as Kullen's were completely satisfied with their work. They were on retainer with a good many clients, something that actually *did* please Rothchild no end.

"Most of our clients tend to be quite sold on us after

they make use of our services." She did her best to go the extra mile for her clients and *none* of them remotely looked as good or seemed as charming as Jackson Wainwright.

Damn it, where had that come from?

His smile only widened, as if he was privy to some private joke he wasn't quite ready to share. "That might be true, but this recommendation, I suspect, started out biased."

"Forgive me, Mr. Wainwright, but I have to ask. Do most banking executives talk in some kind of code the way you do?"

All too often, he was given to beginning sentences in his head and voicing them out loud only when he came to the middle, so he took no offense.

"All right, let me be plain."

"Please." Although she truly doubted that was possible. Men who looked like Jackson Wainwright did didn't even have a nodding acquaintance with the word *plain*. She was fairly certain that Jackson Wainwright was accustomed to women falling all over themselves to garner his favor.

"Your mother recommended you. Well, she recommended both of you, although she didn't mention that K. C. Manetti was actually her daughter. What she did say was that K. C. Manetti and Kullen Manetti were her children."

Her mind had temporarily frozen the moment he'd uttered the word *mother.* Her eyes were on his as she repeated, "My mother."

"Yes." Then, to keep her from asking if perhaps he'd

made a mistake, Jackson described the woman in question to her. "Petite, well-dressed lady. Lively eyes, trim figure, a smile that's rather reminiscent of yours now that I think of it, and—"

For the second time since he'd walked into her office, Kate held up her hand. "My mother, yes, that's her. I get it." What did her mother do, buttonhole every good-looking man she came across and try to steer him directly into her path?

Mother, she silently cried, *you know better.*

Knowing that there would be no peace for her until she knew, Kate had to ask. "What were you doing, talking to my mother?"

"Hiring her actually," Jackson said. "I'm having a small 'get acquainted' party at the bank—I'm the new district manager—and I needed a caterer. Your mother comes very highly recommended. The branch manager had her cater his Christmas party."

Kate had to give her mother that, even though right now, there was a very strong urge to wrap her fingers around her mother's slender neck and just squeeze. Just for a second. Just until she promised never to do this kind of thing again.

When she spoke, restrained anger made Kate's voice sound very formal. "My mother's very good at what she does."

"How about you?" he asked, turning the tables, his eyes pinning her in her place. "Are you very good at what you do?"

She never flinched or looked away. However uncertain she was in her chaotic private life, that was how confident she was in her professional one.

"I am excellent," she assured him. "And I can give you a list of references if you like. Current clients," she added.

Still sitting at her desk, Kate shifted in her chair so she could face her computer. She hit the keyboard, bringing the computer back around from the land of saved watts and slumber. The picture of a beach at sunset faded away and a desktop full of folders popped up. She was about to open one of them when he stopped her.

"Thanks, but don't bother. I like making up my own mind."

She dropped her hand. "And you can do that over lunch." It wasn't a question, just an assumption built on what he'd said a few minutes ago. She did her best to bank down the trace of sarcasm.

He smiled, inclining his head. "Exactly."

If lunch was what he wanted, lunch was what he would get. But not before she had a question of her own answered.

"All right. But before we go, I need to know just what sort of services you'll require."

That really sounded like a loaded question that could be answered in a variety of ways, some of which could get him slapped. Where had that come from? he silently demanded. Granted she was attractive—exceedingly attractive—but that wasn't the reason he was here. What was going on with him?

Maybe, he theorized, he'd been all business for so long, something inside of him was rebelling, trying to break free. Trying to remember what life was all about outside of the pressures of the banking industry.

Or maybe this was his own version of a meltdown. He couldn't honestly say. He *could* say that he had to keep his answer straight and business oriented. Otherwise, there would be repercussions. Serious ones.

"To give you the *Reader's Digest* version, my parents doted on Jonah. He was the firstborn and the golden child. He was—and still can be—very charming and engaging when he wants to be. However, that didn't change the fact that he has a very weak character and my parents eventually had to admit that Jonah had to be saved from himself. So, when they had their will drawn up—they essentially divided the money between Jonah and me—they made sure that his was in the form of a trust fund. Each month a certain amount—generous even by today's standards—would be doled out to Jonah, but the principle would remain intact and in trust until Jonah's thirty-fifth birthday, at which time he would get it all." Jackson paused for a moment, silently wishing that Jonah was the brother he wanted him to be, a brother who didn't need to constantly be reined in or policed. He hated being the bad guy. "Jonah turns thirty-five next month."

It was easy to read between the lines. "And you don't want him inheriting the money."

"No, I don't," Jackson agreed bluntly. "If he gets his

hands on the money, he'll either be dead in a month, or the money'll be gone in six. Or maybe both. If my brother survives, he'll be in debt in seven. It's his nature and although I have bailed him out in the past, his problem keeps mushrooming and eventually, there won't be enough money in the world to cover his debts."

Jackson knew that what he was asking for wasn't easy, nor was it strictly orthodox. Legally, Jonah had every right to expect to finally be united with his inheritance. Jackson was trying to have his parents' wishes and authority usurped by finding a loophole and extending the age limit on the trust. The only reason his parents had picked thirty-five was because they'd honestly believed Jonah would finally get his act together by then.

Surprise, folks. He's still a kid.

He looked at Kate. "Are you up to that, Ms. Manetti, or is it too much of a challenge for your firm?"

Kate raised her chin. "I don't know about my firm, but I enjoy a challenge, Mr. Wainwright."

"Good to hear. All right." On his feet, he rounded the desk and stood beside her chair. "Let's go to lunch."

She'd thought that the matter was settled, despite all his talk about eating. Obviously not. How much more was he going to ask her? Oh well, it *was* lunchtime. She might as well indulge him.

Taking her purse out of the bottom drawer, Kate closed the drawer and rose to her feet. "Am I still auditioning for the part of your lawyer?"

"Yes, you are," he confirmed, deliberately keeping a straight face. But there was a smile in his eyes. "But right now, I'd say you have the inside track on getting the part." She looked at him and it was obvious that she wanted to say something in response. "What?"

Her suspicions had been stirred, but for now, she decided to keep them to herself. "Nothing."

"I require truthfulness at all times."

"All right." She stopped just shy of the door. "Are you really looking for a lawyer?"

"What would I be doing here if I wasn't?"

Infrequent phone calls and contact not withstanding, she knew her mother. Knew how Theresa Manetti thought. Nikki was getting married and she wasn't. Her mother was bent on changing that. Somewhere there was a saint's statue melting because of all the candles that were being lit in front of it. But to ask this man if he'd been sent here to pretend to need her services, all under the guise of meeting and dating her, somehow sounded very conceited. On the chance that she was wrong and he *was* on the level, Kate swallowed her question and forced a smile to her lips.

"You're right," she agreed amiably. "Why would you be here if you didn't need a lawyer?" She glanced at her watch. How did it get to be so late? Especially when it felt as if time was standing still? "If we're going to go to lunch, we'd better get moving."

In his opinion, Theresa Manetti's daughter was moving just fine as it was.

"Your choice," he told her out of the blue. "The restaurant," he explained. "I've been gone a long time and things have changed a lot around Bedford. My favorite restaurant's history, so I leave it up to you to pick one."

"What was your favorite restaurant?" she asked as they walked out of her office.

There was a fond smile on his lips as he said, "Gin-Ling's."

"You like Chinese food?" It was rather a safe deduction.

"I'm rather partial to it, yes."

Well, they had that in common. The next second, she banished the thought from her head. She was *not* going to fall into her mother's trap. "I know a wonderful Chinese restaurant," she told him.

His expression brightened just a shade. "Sounds promising. You can give me the directions when we get to the car."

If nothing else, he thought, holding the door open for her, he was going to get a good meal out of this and perhaps discover a new favorite restaurant.

And if he was lucky, Jackson added silently, he'd wind up getting a very attractive family lawyer to boot.

Things could have been worse.

Chapter Three

Located in the center of an outdoor mall, the China Pearl was a modest-size restaurant that saw more than its fair share of traffic both for lunch and for dinner. There was a bar, small but well stocked, to the right of the entrance and the reservation desk. Four rows of six booths each composed the rest of the floor plan.

After leading them to a booth, the hostess gave them dark green bound menus to peruse and quietly faded back to her post.

Kate pretended to look at the menu. It hadn't changed in over a year. At this point, she knew it by heart. What she didn't know was very much about the man sitting across from her. Was he on the level or the first of an endless line of setups arranged by her mother? A little probing chatter wouldn't be out of order to assess the situation.

"So," she placed the menu on the table in front of her, "are you here in Bedford permanently, or is this just a temporary move until you can straighten things out?"

If it were only that simple, Jackson thought. "Unfortunately, this isn't anything I can put a bandage on," he answered. "I've already tried that. Jonah needs someone in his life on a regular basis, not someone who checks in on him once a week." No matter how many questions he barked into the phone, he thought.

Wainwright seemed to take his responsibility seriously, she thought. Since she'd entered family law, she'd discovered that a lot of people bristled when it came to doing what needed to be done, feeling shackled by "the ties that bind." Was Wainwright just paying lip service in order to make himself look good, or did he really mean what he told her, that he wanted to protect his brother from himself? She supposed it shouldn't really matter to her. Either way, it began to sound as if he really did need a lawyer. Her curiosity was aroused. "That sounds like it can get to be a pretty heavy burden."

Jackson shrugged as he scanned the menu. "It already is. Jonah doesn't like being 'supervised,' he likes being indulged." And that was his parents' fault. Jonah was artistically gifted and, in an attempt to nurture that talent and make it bear fruit, his parents, especially his mother, bent over backward to accommodate Jonah. He loved his brother, but he wasn't about to let him run right over him.

Jackson looked up from the menu. "I'll be honest with you. I've got a feeling that was why Mort suffered his heart attack. The stress of trying to keep my brother in line and out of jail finally got to him."

"Jail?" she asked.

"Disorderly in public," he recited. "Bathing in the fountain in front of city hall at one in the morning—"

"That doesn't sound as if it merited jail."

"Naked," Jackson added.

"Oh. I'd better stock up on blood-pressure medicine, then," Kate quipped. The corners of her mouth curved as she allowed her amusement to surface. "If you don't mind my making an observation, you don't really know how to sell something, do you?"

His eyes held hers. She couldn't quite make up her mind if his were pure blue or if they had a touch of gray in them.

Doesn't matter if they're purple. He's just a client, remember? her inner voice chided.

"I just want you to know up front what you're getting into, Kate," he told her simply. "If you'd rather not have to deal with someone who can make you contemplate justifiable homicide even as he charms the socks off you, I need to know now so I can find someone else to handle this trust-fund restructuring."

"I'm no stranger to contemplating justifiable homicide," she assured him with a smile. "I have a very charming brother of my own."

Their server, a petite young woman in a rich, royal

blue dress with a Mandarin collar and two discreet side slits that stopped just short of the middle of her thigh, brought them a pot of tea and backed away, her silence indicating they could take their time ordering.

Picking up the teapot, Kate filled the two thimble-size cups before them. "Tell me more about Jonah."

Jackson took a breath. Where did he begin? And how did he say this without coming across as bitter? He wasn't bitter, just tired—and losing hope that Jonah would ever come to his senses. "He'll try to charm you into giving him what he wants. If that fails—"

"It will," Kate assured him.

In his experience, women had trouble saying no to Jonah, but he wasn't about to make any assumptions about this new lawyer until he had an opportunity to watch her interact with his brother. "Then he'll try to intimidate you, except that he's not very good at that. Mostly he uses guilt."

"Guilt?"

Jackson nodded. "He wields it like a top-flight surgeon wields a scalpel. He'll make you feel guilty for turning him down. Jonah's very good at manipulating people. He's accumulated a lifetime of experience, working on my parents."

Listening, Kate detected an undercurrent of more than one emotion. His relationship with his brother, she decided, was complicated. "Are you two close?"

Not anymore, Jackson thought. Something else to hold against Jonah. He missed what they'd once had. Missed being proud of his brother instead of drained by him.

He took a sip of tea, letting the warm liquid wind through him before answering. "We were when I was a kid. These days, I'm the bad guy." He laughed shortly. "Jonah's closer to total strangers he hooks up with at clubs than he is to me. There's always someone with him who's his new best friend."

Kate studied Jackson as he spoke, forcing herself to focus on what he said, not the way he looked as he said it. Looks, the crackle of chemistry, none of that mattered anymore, she thought fiercely. It had taken her a long time, but she'd finally learned her lesson. Good-looking men were only hunters and gatherers of women. You couldn't build a stable life with a gatherer.

"You love him a great deal, don't you?" she asked as he paused.

Jackson shrugged, taking another sip. "That has nothing to do with it."

"It's nothing to be embarrassed about," she said matter-of-factly. "If you didn't love your brother, you'd let him get his hands on his share of the inheritance, walk away and go on with your life."

"Maybe I just don't want to be connected to a scandal and if Jonah has free rein to do what he wants with his money, there'll be serious repercussions. I guarantee it. And I'd rather avoid that if I could."

"Understandable," she agreed. "But even a few of our presidents have had to deal with the annoying specter of clueless, classless brothers whose actions kept landing them on page one. They all survived." Kate raised her eyes to his. She considered herself a fairly good judge of character when it came to her clients. She just failed miserably when judging men on a personal level. "You strike me as a man who knows that the people who count will judge him on his own merits."

"Maybe you've forgotten the purpose of this lunch, but it was for me to get to know you, not the other way around."

Amusement curved her mouth. "Things don't always go according to plan."

"No," he agreed, thinking of the life he'd once planned with Rachel. "They certainly don't."

Their server returned, a silent, genial inquiry in her eyes. Kate nodded and ordered first. "I'll have the lobster Cantonese, egg-drop soup and a spring roll."

Inclining her head, the server turned toward Jackson.

He hadn't made his selection yet. Hearing what Kate ordered, he decided to go with that. "That sounds good," he said to the server, surrendering his menu. "Make that two."

The young woman smiled, nodded and retreated with their menus.

Kate folded her hands before her. "All right, what would you like to know?" she asked the moment their server had left.

What you'd look like, waking up beside me in the morning.

He had no idea where that had come from. He did know that he would have felt more comfortable if his lawyer had been less attractive. Or a man. It was hard to keep his mind on business when the sight of her kept ushering in completely unrelated stray thoughts.

"What would you like to tell me?" he asked politely.

She poured more tea into her cup, then raised it to her lips, buying herself some time.

This was an odd way to conduct a first interview, she thought. Wainwright had placed control, at least temporarily, back in her hands. Was that to make her feel comfortable? Or to get her to relax before he sprang his real questions on her?

And then there was that tiny, nagging thought. Her mother had sent him. There was still a possibility, growing smaller now she had to admit, that this was all a setup.

"That if you're looking for a good lawyer, I won't disappoint you." Then, in case he thought she was bragging, Kate gave him a little background information. "My brother and I are third-generation lawyers. My father helped found this firm. *His* father was a criminal lawyer. Grandpa had his own one-man practice," she elaborated. "Most of the time he defended people who, without him, would have had nowhere to turn for proper representation. I'm not afraid of hard work," she continued. "My brother will tell you that arguing's in my blood. If you decided to go with my firm—with me—I'll do my very best to accomplish whatever you ask me to."

The last line hung in the air between them and she prayed he couldn't interpret that the wrong way, because suddenly, they sounded like a sensual promise to her ear. What was wrong with her? She was usually sharper than that.

Taking a breath, she delivered her closing argument. "And if you're afraid that your brother will sweet-talk me into bending the rules for him, don't be. You pay the bills, you get to make the calls," she assured him. "I'm just the instrument that makes whatever you require done come true."

"An instrument, eh?" he repeated. The analogy amused him, but he made no further comment on it. He had a more important question. "Do you really think that you can keep Jonah's trust fund safe?"

"Yes," she said confidently.

"How?"

"It won't be the easiest thing to overhaul," she admitted. "But I think there's a way around it. Your parents initially had the trust fund drawn up because they didn't consider Jonah mature enough to manage his own money, right?"

"That about sums it up," he told her.

"If I can show that Jonah's maturity level hasn't progressed to the level of an average thirty-five-year-old man, the level your parents felt was right to finally allow him to have control over his share of the money, we might be able to push the time limit back, make it more flexible by specifying that certain conditions have to be met. And if they're not met, the present arrangement of giving him a certain amount every month will continue. Indefinitely," she concluded.

"And just how do you intend to accomplish that?" he pressed.

"By compiling reports on your brother's irresponsible behavior—interviewing his friends, any officers who might have been called in because of complaints by his neighbors or who issued tickets for reckless driving, things like that. It gives us a leg to stand on. I can submit the report to a judge and have the trust sustained," she told him. She expected Jackson to express relief. Instead, she saw a frown forming on his lips. "Is something wrong?"

He was thinking of the repercussions of filing this sort of a report. "I don't want him to be publicly humiliated."

"Doesn't have to be publicly," she assured him. "It just has to go to a sympathetic judge." He needed more, she thought. He really *did* care for his brother. "I won't do anything without first running it by you. Fair enough?"

He nodded. "Fair enough." Their server was back. As she divvied up the different plates, placing a small bowl of soup before each of them, the conversation was temporarily tabled. When she left, Jackson said to Kate, "You've got the job."

Kate had already assumed that she had, but she thanked him politely for the confirmation, then went on to tell him, "I'm going to need all the papers from the original trust fund filing as soon as possible."

"I'll have to look for them." He thought for a moment, trying to remember where his copy was. His best bet was to secure the copy that had to still be in Mort's

office. The late family lawyer had to be the most orga-
nized man he'd ever met. "Soon as I get my hands on
them, I'll have a courier bring them to your office. Better
yet, why don't you come by Republic National's corporate offices this Friday after five and I'll hand them
over to you personally?" Because she looked slightly
puzzled at the time he mentioned, Jackson explained,
"That party I'm having your mother cater, it's set for
Friday in our conference room. It's meant to be a kind
of icebreaker to get better acquainted with the people
who'll be working for me. It'll be nice to have someone
there who *doesn't* work for me." He smiled at the
thought.

"Technically speaking," Kate pointed out, "you're
my boss."

He wasn't deterred. "Then, for the evening, we won't
speak technically." His voice softened a little. "I need a
friendly face I can trust to be honest," he said. "It'll
help me relax."

"Wouldn't want you tense," she murmured. *Or me,
either,* she added silently. And she was despite all her
best efforts not to be.

Kate lost more time than she'd intended to. It was a
few minutes after four when she finally got back to her
office. After having lunch with her new client—there
was no way she was giving him back to Kullen after
laying this much groundwork—she had him drive her
back not to the office but to its parking structure.

Once there, she had just enough time to dash to her own car and drive off to the county courthouse. She already had all the papers she needed in order to file for Mrs. Greenfeld's official name change. She'd packed them earlier in a spare briefcase she had locked in the trunk of her car.

The simple task took close to two hours thanks to the fact that the courtroom was packed. Nothing new there. While she entertained the idea of just going home from there, she had too much waiting for her on her desk. With a sigh, she drove back to the Bedford-based firm. With any luck, she'd be able to go home by six.

But probably not.

Sinking into her ergonomically designed leather chair, Kate barely had time to let out a long sigh before Kullen stuck his head in.

A feeling of déjà vu slid over her.

"So, how did it go?" he asked cheerfully, closing the door behind him. He took a couple of steps in, then stopped to study her and see how receptive she was. He wanted to be ready for a quick escape, should the need for that arise. Because he knew his mother had sent this new client to them and had expressly told him to make sure that Kate was the one who took him on as a client.

Kate glared at him. "I shouldn't even talk to you."

He winced. "That bad, huh?"

She shook her head. "No, actually it wasn't bad at all."

"So he was good-looking?"

That caught her up short. Kullen had never met with

Wainwright so he would have no idea what he looked like. "That has nothing to do with it. Why would you even ask that?"

Not wanting to let on that their mother had mentioned that little fact, he glossed over it and shrugged. "You know me, I'm always saying sexist things."

"Did Mom put you up to your vanishing act?"

He almost asked how she knew but managed to catch himself in time. "No, I told you, Sheila accidentally scheduled both appointments at the same time. Thanks to your being such a workaholic, I was able to keep my original appointment."

Kate saw right through that. Her eyes narrowed, pinning her brother in place. "With Allison?"

He would have denied it if he'd thought that it would work. But he knew it was useless. Somehow, Kate *always* knew when he wasn't on the level with her. "Why can't I lie to you?"

Kate laughed, shaking her head. "God knows it's not for lack of trying on your part. But I know you too well. I know all your tells."

"Tells?" he echoed.

"Your nostrils flare when you lie." She frowned, thinking of the woman her brother had just wasted time with. "I thought that by now you would have moved on from that bimbo."

Humor curved his mouth, even as he tried to sound serious. "Have a little respect, you're speaking of the bimbo I love."

She sincerely doubted that her brother had ever been in love. The strongest emotion he'd probably ever experienced was infatuation. "At least for today."

"All any of us have, Katie, is the moment," he deadpanned.

Kate sighed. Maybe she didn't get out these days, but her brother got out *too* much, spreading himself incredibly thin. His time could be so much better spent.

"Honestly, Kullen, I don't know what you see in that woman. I've removed lint from the dryer that's more intelligent than she is."

"I'm not really interested in giving her an IQ test."

He was better than that, Kate silently insisted. She knew if she'd said it out loud, her brother would deny it. "You are impossible, Kullen."

"But happy," he countered with a broad smile. "Very, very happy. You really should try it once in a while, Kate."

She could feel her guard going up. "What? Going out with Allison?"

"No," he said seriously, "being happy. Not every guy out there is a rotten SOB."

No, only the ones I'm attracted to. Kate closed her eyes for a second, gathering strength. "Don't you start sounding like Mom."

"Hey, her heart's in the right place." He started to open the door again.

"Remember that when she suddenly starts working on you."

He paused to look at her over his shoulder. The grin on his face was utterly boyish. Kate could readily see why, at any given time, there were so many women pursuing her brother. He had a face that could stop a heart and fill it full of longing.

"She'd have to catch me first. Besides, you're her pet project for now and given your 'willingness' to cooperate, I'd say Mom is going to be busy for a very long time."

Kate pointed to the door. "Get out of here."

He was on his way out, but he needled her a little more. "Stop scowling, Katie. You know you can't stay mad at me."

"This time around, I intend to give it a real good try," she informed him. But as her brother walked out, she raised her voice and called after him, "Don't forget, you owe me."

He half turned in the doorway. "Say what?"

"I said you owe me."

"My undying love," he replied. "After that, we'll talk."

"You owe me for taking on your client," she said pointedly.

Curiosity got the better of him. "So this was actually on the level? He really does need a lawyer?"

"Oddly enough, yes, he was on the level."

Kullen laughed shortly to himself. "She found a legitimate one to send. Mom's good."

Easy for him to say. "I'll remind you of that when it's your turn."

The wide grin was back. "Never happen."

"Don't underestimate that little woman," Kate warned him, thinking back to the days not all that long ago when her mother was actively lobbying for her to get married. "When she makes up her mind about something, she clamps down harder than a junkyard dog."

"She'll have to corner me first," Kullen crowed just before he closed the door behind him.

Oh, she will, Kullen, Kate silently promised with more than a little confidence. *She will.*

Chapter Four

Kate had every intention of calling her mother and letting her know that she didn't appreciate being manipulated like this. But the phone on her desk rang just as she reached for it. She was wanted in a general meeting. For the time being, anything private had to be pushed to the side. Kate promised herself to make the call to her mother when she got home.

But by the time she got home, all Kate had the strength to do was crawl into bed.

The following day was just as packed, with no letup in sight. And then, somehow, it was Friday and she had her newest client's function to attend.

Looking back, Kate wasn't even sure why she'd agreed

to go. It really wasn't to get those papers she needed to start the extension on the trust because they could have come just as easily—and more efficiently—by courier as she'd first suggested.

Maybe, that annoying little voice in her head speculated, she'd said yes to Jackson's invitation because she was ever so slightly attracted to the man. Be that as it may—and he *was* attractive—she planned to fight that attraction with her very last ounce of strength.

It had taken her a long time to get herself together. She was drained and very tired of the so-called dating game. Tired of putting herself out there emotionally only to have her hopes dashed over and over again by men who didn't turn out to be worth the effort. She'd actually thought that she'd finally hit the mother lode with Matthew. The man was handsome, intelligent, sharp and ambitious. He seemed perfect in every way. Not only that, but there was chemistry. Oh God, there was chemistry, that magic "something" that made her tingle whenever she was near him.

She didn't trust chemistry, not anymore. It had blinded her to things she might have noticed sooner—like the fact that Matthew turned out to have a ten-feet-tall libido.

No, no more chemistry for her. No more men, period. At least, not socially.

To that end, when she'd gotten up this morning, Kate had had every intention to dress the part of a subdued, scholarly professional. That usually made her look years older than she actually was. And that, in turn, would show Mr. Wainwright that theirs was nothing more than strictly a professional relationship.

But somewhere between the shower, the closet and the eyebrow pencil, the rebellious side of her kicked in. The side that liked testing her and pushing her to her limits, no matter what the case. So, rather than pin her hair back or up, the way she did when she was due in court, Kate wore it loose, letting the natural curl take over. Her hair looked like a black storm at sea.

She still chose a suit to wear, but it wasn't one of her more somber ones. This suit was an eye-opening turquoise. The pencil skirt was teasingly shorter than the one she'd worn when she'd had lunch with Jackson. The hem found its place somewhere along her thigh rather than her knee, exposing very shapely legs. The blouse was a satiny shade of cream.

And just before she left, she took a pair of cream-colored strappy heels with her. They were a full inch higher than the ones she usually wore to the office.

All in all, she looked like Hollywood's idea of a lady lawyer in a romantic comedy—and she knew it. What wasn't clear was why she was doing it.

Catching a glimpse of herself in the downstairs dining-room mirror, Kate hesitated. If she wasn't running late this morning, she would have hurried back up the stairs and changed into her usual somber apparel.

Or so she told herself as she dashed out the door.

* * *

"Hey, you look pretty good," Kullen observed as, nine hours later, she passed him in the hall on her way to attend Wainwright's gathering.

Kate stopped for a moment and looked at him. "You sound surprised."

"I am," he admitted. "I forget how good you can look when you're not trying to impress Rothchild with your brains."

He was referring to her father's edict that men didn't believe that a woman could be both attractive and smart. If she wanted to get somewhere in this field, her father had told her that she would have to pick which way she wanted to be perceived. Pretty or intelligent.

Because her father so seldom went out of his way to mentor her in any fashion—that sort of thing he saved for Kullen—she took his words to heart and made her choice. She picked smart and the subdued clothes that went with that.

But because she didn't want to hear any of Kullen's pseudo-intellectual observations, she pretended not to understand. "I'm not even going to try to unscramble that. I'm just going to take my compliment and leave."

"Speaking of which," his eyes swept over her again with even more interest than the first time, "where are you leaving to?"

She wasn't about to surrender information so easily. "Maybe I'm going home."

Kullen shook his head. "Not looking like that you're not. You got a date, Katie?" he asked incredulously.

It had been a long day and her temper had grown shorter by the hour. She had little patience left for Kullen's inquisition. "What, Mom has you spying for her now?"

"Ever think that maybe *I'm* concerned about you?" There wasn't even a glimmer of a smile on his lips.

She knew he cared about her, as she did him. But that didn't mean that he would miss a chance to bedevil her. "Nope. It never occurred to me."

Kullen placed a hand dramatically over his heart. "I'm wounded."

"You'll heal," she assured him. "Don't forget to get your bimbo shots. Prolonged exposure to bimbos causes wounds to fester," she tossed over her shoulder as she turned a corner and came to the bank of elevators.

Behind her, in the distance, she heard the sound of her brother's deep laughter.

Well, at least one of Theresa Manetti's children was happy, Kate thought.

Half an hour later, after crawling through rush-hour traffic, she left her car in the parking structure across the street from the bank. It had taken her thirty minutes to go ten blocks.

The Republic National's building was twelve years old and, at its inception, had been the last word in modern. It still was.

Standing fifteen stories tall, every one of its floors

was filled with offices that were in some way connected with the bank. Impressive by day, with the sun reflecting off each one of its carpet-to-ceiling glass-framed floors, the building was even more impressive at night with the rays of the full moon glinting off its otherwise darkened windows.

The building looked beautiful, but cold, Kate thought, approaching the edifice.

The description echoed in her brain.

Was that how people saw her? She knew without conceit that she was attractive. Knew it in the same way that she knew her eyes were a deep blue. She hadn't done anything to make them blue, they just were. So it was with being attractive. Yes, she spent time in the morning putting on makeup, but it was just a smattering. Nothing earth-shaking or image-changing. She was what she was and she was satisfied with that.

Why was she even thinking about this? she upbraided herself. Her mother, she thought. Her mother had started this by playing matchmaker.

Sorry, Mom, that ship no longer docks here.

She had to walk past a security desk in the lobby before reaching the bank of elevators. Kate paused to sign in. Again she briefly entertained the idea of just turning around and going back out. She could offer some excuse to Wainwright about having something come up at the last minute—it wasn't that much of a stretch, things were *always* coming up.

But at bottom, she knew that would be running and

Anthony Manetti's daughter didn't run. It was as simple—and as complicated—as that.

Besides, Kate silently asked herself as she stepped into the elevator car, what was she afraid of? She knew damn well what happened if she gave in to chemistry, so she wouldn't. There was nothing to be afraid of, she silently insisted.

Her stomach tightened as the floors went by.

The conference room had recently been remodeled. Among other things, the east wall had been taken down, merging it with the other conference room and creating a single room that was twice as large. It was a show of confidence to its employees that they expected better economic times to be just on the horizon.

Aside from the regular conferences, the room could now handily accommodate social gatherings at Christmas and other festive times of the year. It was certainly large enough to hold all the department heads and their people without anyone being forced to literally rub elbows.

All but awash in milling bodies the moment she walked into the conference room, Kate took the opportunity to acclimate herself. Was Jackson really in charge of all these people? He looked almost too young for that sort of responsibility. But then, she supposed that being forced to be his brother's keeper had left him little time for a carefree life.

She scanned the area for his face.

* * *

He saw her the moment she walked in.

Jackson stopped in mid-sentence as the elevator announced its appearance with a distinctive bell. He glanced in its direction each time he heard the bell. Two beats later, his family lawyer, true to her word, entered.

But with a hell of a difference. Even though that was what she was, Jackson found it difficult to think of Kate Manetti as his new family lawyer. She was far too vivacious to be a straitlaced lawyer. Or even a terrific lawyer.

If Jonah saw her, he would do his damndest to try to add the woman to his trophies. Jackson suddenly felt very protective of her.

"Excuse me," he murmured to Ed Wynters, the man he'd been speaking to. He placed his wineglass on the table. "I see someone I need to talk to."

Wynters, the vice president of Equity Loans, turned around to see who the new district manager was referring to. A wide smile flittered over the VP's portly face.

"I'd need to talk to her, too, if I wasn't such a happily married man," he added with just a touch of a sorrowful note lingering on the last three words.

Jackson didn't offer a response. He was already weaving his way toward her.

"You made it," Jackson said when he reached her. Instinctively he sensed that she wouldn't have wanted any undue attention directed her way, which was why he hadn't shouted his greeting from across the room.

Kate turned to the sound of his voice. "I said I would," she reminded him, conveniently omitting mentioning that she'd almost turned around twice while en route. All he needed to know was that she was here, not the indecision that had marked her path.

"Yes," he acknowledged, "I remember. But a great many things can happen between 'yesterday' and 'today' to change that."

That hit a little too close to the truth for her comfort. Wavering and uncertain was not the kind of aura she wanted to project publicly *or* privately.

"Luckily, they didn't." She took a breath and forced a smile to her lips. "So, did you bring the papers with you?"

"Don't tell me you intend to grab and run. Stay a few minutes," he coaxed, slipping a hand lightly to her waist and guiding her in the direction of the buffet table. "Enjoy the food. It's really excellent." He realized he was praising her mother and laughed at himself for forgetting. "But then, you'd already know that, wouldn't you?"

"Yes, I would know that." Her mother was an excellent cook, there was no denying that. The woman's flaws came under the heading of motherhood. Theresa Manetti really needed to learn to butt out unless her opinion was specifically requested.

As she spoke to Jackson, Kate couldn't shake the uneasy feeling that she was being watched. She scanned the room, trying to locate her mother. Because of all the people milling around, getting in the way, it was impossible to see everywhere.

And somewhere in all this, Kate would have bet a year's salary, her mother was lurking. Theresa Manetti made it a rule to be on site for every party she catered in order to make sure that everything went smoothly— and to do damage control if it didn't.

But if her mother knew she was here, Kate suspected that the woman would probably be trying to keep a very low profile.

Come out, come out wherever you are. You can't hide forever, Mother.

Abruptly, Kate realized that her newest client was asking her a question. Forcing a smile to her lips, she turned her attention to him.

"I'm sorry, I thought I saw someone I knew. I didn't. You were saying?"

"Would you like something to drink?" Jackson gestured toward the minibar that had been set up just beyond the buffet table. "The bar looks small, but it has just about anything you might want."

She caught herself sparing a side glance in his direction. The words *I don't know about that* popped up in her head out of nowhere. Recovering, she was just grateful they hadn't emerged on her tongue, as well.

Out loud, she dismissed the offer. "I'm driving."

"Not this minute," Jackson countered.

"No," she agreed, holding her ground like a soldier, more stubborn than brave, "but in a few."

"Stay," he coaxed in a voice that could have just as easily been used for seduction. "I thought of a few more things to ask you."

It was an excuse made out of tissue paper. But, even knowing that, Kate allowed herself to be led to the bar. So what could it hurt to stay awhile? After this, she was going home and nothing pressing awaited her.

"A screwdriver," she told the man behind the bar.

Jackson's eyes slid up from her toes to her face, taking a prolonged route up. She could almost feel him doing it.

"Nothing more exotic?" he asked her.

Why was it suddenly warm in here? Had a few hundred more people been brought in? Or was the oxygen being sucked out? she wondered nervously.

"I don't need anything more exotic," she managed to answer as the heat evaporated the saliva from her mouth. "I like screwdrivers."

"I'll try to remember that," he replied.

Why did that sound like a promise?

The cold glass when the bartender handed it to her felt exceptionally good in her hand.

"Mrs. Manetti, I'm running out of napkins," Eva, a pretty little redhead, declared as she approached the woman who was all but a patron saint in her eyes. Because of Theresa Manetti, she was in a position to accumulate enough money to allow her to pay for her second year of college instead of dropping out.

"There're more in the truck, Eva." Pausing, Theresa fished out her car keys from her pocket. She held them out to the girl. "Here, take Jeffrey with you and go get them. The truck's parked in the basement directly by the elevator."

Eva's smile was tolerant. "I don't need Jeffrey to come with me, Mrs. Manetti. I can get the napkins by myself."

"It's after hours in an office building and you're a very attractive young woman." Theresa patted the girl's cheek with affection. The young were fearless. The not-so-young knew there was an underbelly that wasn't always so nice. "Better safe than sorry, my dear. Humor me. Take Jeffrey with you."

There was affection in Eva's voice as she said, "You worry too much."

Theresa laughed softly. "My daughter tells me that all the time."

"My mother never tells me that," Eva confided. She considered for a moment, then said, "I like you worrying, Mrs. Manetti. I'll take Jeffrey."

"That's my girl."

When Theresa looked back to where she'd first spotted her daughter standing, talking to Jackson, Kate was no longer there. And neither was Jackson. She could only hope that they had slipped away together. The next moment, another one of the servers she'd hired was asking her about one of the trays of appetizers.

Before she knew it, Theresa had lost herself in the dozen and a half details that always arose at a catering function, all of which demanded her attention.

"So what are those questions you wanted to ask me?" Kate prodded. Several minutes had gone by and they had all been immersed in small talk and an undercurrent of

flirtation on Jackson's part. She couldn't help responding to him. In her defense, any woman with a pulse
would have. As long as she didn't allow herself to take
it seriously, she'd be fine.

He smiled into her eyes over his drink. "Are you
always this focused?"

She was caught up in a verbal version of dodgeball,
she thought. Well, two could play that game. "Is that one
of the questions or something that just occurred to you
on the spur of the moment?" she asked.

His gaze made her warmer. She shouldn't have had
a sip of the screwdriver. That didn't help matters any.
"Would there be different answers depending on the
circumstances?"

All right, she'd play along. And then maybe he'd
give her those papers. "I'm here as your lawyer," she
emphasized, "so yes, I try to always be this focused."

"And if I'd asked you to come here not as my lawyer
but as an extremely attractive woman, then would you
be this focused?"

Because the intensity of his gaze had caused her
mouth to go dry, she didn't answer until she took
another sip of her drink. A long one. "But I'm here
to pick up your papers. The ones to enable me to
extend the life of your brother's trust fund, remember? That would make me your lawyer, not your
guest."

"Could you forget about the trust fund for the next
few hours?" he requested. "This is the beginning of the

weekend. There's no need for you to work on anything until Monday morning."

She had to remind herself to breathe. *Not good.*

Clearing her throat, Kate forced the words out. "I like to stay ahead of things," she informed him. "That means sometimes not just burning the midnight oil but the weekend one, too."

His smile found its way to each and every one of her bones, threatening to melt at least half of them. "Well, I'm certainly glad your mother gave me your number and your brother turned out not to be available. I'm obviously getting my money's worth. Speaking of which—"

She'd lost the reference point. "Money?" Kate asked uncertainly.

"No," he laughed. "Your mother." He pointed to the left with his glass. "She's right over there."

Kate turned and saw the woman. Eye contact was definitely established. "So she is."

When Kate made no move either to wave at the woman or walk over to her, Jackson's curiosity was aroused. "Are you two not on speaking terms?"

"She's working. I don't want to break her concentration." And yelling at her mother would definitely break her concentration, Kate added silently.

"So this is why you couldn't lend me the money when I asked you to the other day."

The accusation came from behind them. Jackson and Kate turned around simultaneously, although Jackson didn't really have to. He knew who it was.

"I'm hurt, little brother. You didn't invite me to this little party you're throwing. But you can make amends," the man said magnanimously. His eyes washed over her in a slow, obviously appreciative motion. Kate felt as if her clothes had just been melted away. She resisted the urge to throw her hands up around herself to cover her nakedness. "You can introduce me to this magnificent creature."

Kate instinctively knew this had to be Jonah.

Chapter Five

Tension traveled through Jackson's shoulders, making them rigid. He braced himself for a scene. Jonah knew where he worked, but his brother hadn't known anything about the get-acquainted party that he'd decided to throw. Was he here at this time by accident, or had he turned up with some kind of agenda?

"Jonah, this isn't the time," he told his brother quietly.

"Oh, but this is exactly the time, little brother," Jonah assured him. His eyes never left Kate. "Now, tell me, just who is this lovely creature and how did you get lucky enough to meet her?"

Jackson looked at her as if he was asking her permission to make the introduction under these circumstances.

She inclined her head ever so slightly, intrigued by Jackson's reaction. Just like that, Kate thought, Jackson Wainwright had turned from a sensual man into a protective one. She had to admit she rather liked that quality in a man.

Careful, Kate, don't lose your focus.

Ever so subtly, Jackson guided them to a lesser trafficked corner. "Jonah, this is our new lawyer, Katherine Manetti. Kate, this is Jonah, my older brother."

Jonah took the hand she extended in greeting, slipping it between both of his.

The dark brown eyes momentarily shifted from her face. "I'm always open to making the acquaintance of a beautiful woman, but why do we need a lawyer?" he asked, sparing his brother a glance. "Or are you the one who needs one? Planning on needing a lawyer to defend you from charges of embezzlement, little brother?"

"She'll be taking Mort's place, Jonah."

"Ah, yes." Nodding, Jonah continued holding her hand. "Mortie." Jonah leaned in toward her, dropping his voice as if to share some kind of dark secret with her. "Poor Mortie has gone to the big courtroom in the sky. Or wherever it is that useless, annoying lawyers go." He beamed at her and she had to admit, the man had a very disarming smile. Like his brother. "No offense, lovely lady, but why would we need another of Mortie's kind?" The question was directed to his brother even though he was still watching Kate. "All he ever did was oversee that stupid trust fund like an iron-fisted troll. His time with us would have been up next month anyway. I turn the magic age then, remember, Jackson?"

"I remember," Jackson replied, holding his emotions in check. "That's exactly why we need Kate."

Jonah's mouth curved slyly. "Oh, I can think of a lot of reasons we—at least I—could need Kate here. And that damn constricting trust fund has absolutely nothing to do with it."

"That's enough, Jonah," Jackson ordered.

Jonah hardly paid attention to the warning note in his brother's voice. "No, not by a long shot. I'm just getting started." His eyes all but shone.

"Jonah, I think that it's time for you to—"

Jackson was going to tell his brother to leave, Kate thought. She could see the whole scenario unfolding, the one that she was certain Jackson would have really wanted to avoid. Slipping her hand out of Jonah's, she deftly moved between the two men and deliberately focused her attention on the older of the two.

"Since I'm your lawyer, Jonah, why don't we go somewhere where you can talk more freely and get acquainted?" she suggested.

Jonah grinned like a small boy who'd just trumped his brother. He glanced over Kate's head at Jackson. "Sorry, little brother, looks like the lady prefers charm to intelligence."

She was making a mistake, Jackson thought. She had

no idea what Jonah was like. Or what, once drunk, he was capable of. "Kate, you don't have to—"

Her arm threaded through Jonah's, Kate turned her head toward Jackson. "I always make it a point to know the person I'm representing, Mr. Wainwright," she informed him very formally.

The expression in her eyes told him it was better if he backed off—and that she knew what she was doing.

Logic warred with chivalry. Jackson had been here for only a few weeks. He'd specifically thrown this party to integrate himself with these people and have them see him in the right light. This was *not* the time or place to have any dirty laundry aired. He hoped that she knew what she was doing.

"There's a coffee shop at the end of the block," she continued, talking to Jonah again. "Why don't we go there?"

"My place isn't that far," Jonah told her, his meaning crystal clear.

It'll be a cold day in hell before that happens, Jonah, she silently vowed.

"Yes, but the coffee shop is right here," Kate countered. "Might as well take advantage of that." *Instead of me.*

Jonah let a small sigh escape. "The coffee shop," he repeated with a resigned nod.

Jackson knew what she was doing and he didn't like it. Jonah was his problem. No need for her to have to put up with him, other than to provide the legal muscle.

"Kate—"

"Face it, Jackie, she's made her choice," Jonah crowed.

With that, secure in the way her arm was tucked through his, Jonah led her back to the elevator. It arrived almost the moment he pressed the button.

Kate deliberately slipped her arm out of his as she stepped into the elevator. She had no intention of being sealed to his side a moment longer than was absolutely necessary.

Although she maintained a smile on her lips, she tendered Jonah a warning. "You're not to embarrass him in public like that again, Jonah."

Jonah's grin broadened, and he seemed somewhat impressed. "Whoa, the lady has a bite. I like ladies with spirit."

They reached the ground floor in the blink of an eye. Pausing to sign out, Kate turned to him and asked, "Why do you do that?"

Jonah scribbled his name on the line after hers and then pushed the outer door open for her. "Do what?"

Kate led him to the right. The coffee shop was only a few steps away. Several of the outdoor tables were occupied. But one or two were still free. "Why do you act like a caricature of the drunken black sheep of the family?"

They went inside the shop. Only one person was in front of them.

Jonah shrugged in response to her question. "Maybe because I am."

Giving her order to the man behind the counter, Kate waited until Jonah followed suit before discounting his answer. "There's more to you than that."

"Want to unwrap the layers? I'll stand real still," he promised, doing his best to sound lecherous.

Their coffees were mixed and ready. Jonah paid and they sat down at an outdoor table. She took a sip of the bracing drink.

"Did you know that your brother has a painting of yours in his office?" she asked.

The look on Jonah's face told her he thought she was making it up. He never stopped to ask how she knew that he painted. "No, he doesn't."

"Yes, he does," she countered. "I've seen it. It's the one of the art fair at Laguna Beach," she added in case he still didn't believe her. "You've got a lot of talent, Jonah." She studied him for a moment. "Maybe you're afraid of that talent," she guessed. "Afraid to work at it. If you never push to succeed, you never have to deal with finding out if you can. So instead, you do this. You do things to excess."

He shrugged carelessly, staring down at the coffee container as if he wished he had something stronger to pour into it. "And maybe you're a frustrated pseudo-psychiatrist."

His tone was harsh, but she didn't pull back. Kate saw the retort for what it was, a fearful response. She'd hit a nerve. Jonah was a lost boy who tried to cover up his shortcomings with an abrasive swagger.

"Your brother went through a lot of trouble to move down here so he could keep an eye on you."

Jonah grew defensive. And annoyed. "Nobody asked him to."

"True," she agreed. "But maybe he knows a cry for help when he hears it."

"Nobody cried, either," Jonah informed her tersely. Then he softened, smiling again. "You're right. My brother is a good guy and he has put up with a lot from me."

She got the feeling that Jonah wanted to do better, he just didn't know how. "So why don't you take pity on him and give him a break?"

The grin grew wider. "He expects it. I've got a reputation to maintain. Being a screwup is what I do best."

"You don't mean that," she told him.

He shrugged in a self-deprecating manner. "Oh yes I do."

"It doesn't have to be that way," she said softly.

Not wanting to continue in this venue, Jonah changed the course of the conversation. "Once I get what's coming to me, Jackson doesn't have to hear from me at all if he doesn't want to."

She studied Jonah a moment longer, then asked, "What do you plan to do with the money once the trust is awarded to you?"

There was a full, robust enthusiasm in his voice as he declared, "Enjoy it."

"You mean spend it," Kate interpreted.

He laughed at her attempt to make the situation more significant than it was. "That's one way to do it. Want to come along? I could use some gorgeous eye candy hanging on to my arm while I sail through the high life. It's a lot of money," he confided with a wink. "But then, you probably already know that."

Actually, she didn't know the specifics, not yet. Kate continued studying him as she sipped her ice blend mocha coffee. "What are you going to do once the money's gone?"

The shrug was careless and completely honest in its lack of guile. "That won't happen for a while. I'll worry about it then." A touch of impatience entered Jonah's voice. He didn't like resistance. It didn't make him play harder. It made him give up. "You know, you might not look like him, but you're a lot like Jackson. Worrying about stuff that's in the future. The future's just that, in the future. Who knows, I might be dead before I run out of money."

She thought of what Jackson had said about his brother's penchant for substance abuse and hanging around unsavory characters.

"That might very well be," she agreed. "But you don't want to do that."

"Right now," he said, leaning close, "what I want is to get my toes warmed by a very gorgeous, classy-looking woman," he breathed.

Kate never flinched, treating him like an over enthusiastic puppy. "Tempting as that sounds, you're my client, Jonah. There are rules."

"I'm not," he protested. "Jackson is."

"Actually," she corrected, "you both are." For now, there was no need to tell him any more detail than that.

Jonah sighed. Anything he had to work for to win wasn't worth the effort. "So you're saying no?"

"I'm saying no for ethical reasons." Her smile never wavered.

"Too bad." His disappointment sounded genuine. "We would have had one hell of a night."

It cost her nothing to leave his ego intact. "I'm sure we would have."

Jonah brightened like a man who believed he was getting what he wanted after all. "Well then, why don't we—"

"I'd be disbarred, Jonah," she emphasized. Her coffee finished, she wiped her lips lightly, then stuffed the napkin into the empty container. "Can I call you a cab?" she suggested.

Jonah eyed her quizzically through the fog in his eyes. "Why? Am I going somewhere?"

"To your house."

"But my car—" He pointed vaguely in the direction he'd last left the parking structure. It had moved. Or the earth had. Either way, he realized he was pointing at a jewelry store.

"—will still be there tomorrow." No way was she allowing him to drive himself to the bathroom, much less out on the road. He reeked of alcohol. "You don't want to risk getting a DUI, possibly hurting yourself or someone else, do you?"

His grin was slightly sloppy now. "Why, Katie, you care."

"I looked into your record. Your brother's pulled a lot of strings to keep you from being sent to jail on drunk and disorderly charges."

"Yeah, good ol' Jackie, he always comes through. He deserves better," he confided.

She made no comment. They'd already run this go-around. "One day he's going to run out of strings and you're going to wind up out of luck. My advice is that you quit while you're ahead."

"You're not as much fun as you look," Jonah lamented as he nodded at her words.

Kate laughed shortly. "I've been told that," she admitted. By princes who turned out to be frogs, she thought, reminding herself why she'd sworn off the species.

Seeing a cab let off a fare across the street, Kate whistled loudly and waved her hand to get the man's attention. She succeeded.

Jonah ambled over from their table. "That's pretty impressive," he commented.

"My brother taught me," she told him matter-of-factly, leaving out the part about badgering Kullen for weeks until he finally gave in.

The cab she'd hailed went down to the end of the street and did a U-turn, coming back to them.

"Your ride's here," Kate informed the unsteady Jonah cheerfully as she opened the rear passenger door for him. With a resigned sigh, Jonah came forward and started to get into the cab. "Watch your head," she cautioned, placing her hand over the top of it as he ducked into the taxi.

Once seated, he peered out at her hopefully. "Sure you don't want to come with me?"

She kept her smile in place. "I'm sure." Moving to the driver, she rattled off Jonah's address for the man, something else she'd committed to memory. She looked in on him one last time. His eyes were getting droopy. She'd made the right call.

"Sleep it off, Jonah," she instructed by way of a parting.

"I'd rather sleep with you," he called out the open window as the cab driver sped away.

"Not even in your wildest dreams," Kate murmured, stepping back on the curb.

For a fleeting moment, she thought about going back upstairs to Jackson's party. She still didn't have the papers that she'd come for. But running interference for Jackson and getting Jonah to go home without, accidentally or on purpose, causing a scene had left her drained.

She could always get the papers on Monday, she decided. Kate turned toward the parking structure and started to walk. At least she'd managed to divert a minor disaster and she'd gotten to meet the black sheep—who was more gray than black. What a handful he must have been for Jackson, she mused, feeling more than a little sorry for the younger Wainwright. It spoke well of him to have taken it on.

He doesn't need you to write a testimonial for him.
She was going to have to keep her guard up all the time,

Kate schooled herself. Otherwise, she would find herself sliding down a very familiar slope—and she knew how that always ended up.

Entering the parking structure, Kate squared her shoulders. She absolutely hated looking for her vehicle. It was never where she was sure she'd left it. Hunting for it took anywhere from fifteen minutes to an hour.

Tonight was no different.

As she pulled up in the driveway, visions of a hot bubble bath proved too seductively tempting for her to resist. Since she was home earlier than she expected, she would take advantage of that and get some overdue sleep. She'd earned it, she told herself. And then some.

But Kate had no sooner closed the door behind her, locking it, and kicked off her shoes than the doorbell rang.

Surprised, she jumped. Now what? she wondered impatiently.

She wasn't expecting anyone, but Kullen had a habit of dropping by without warning. Although never on a Friday night. For a second, she held her ground, waiting to see if whoever it was went away. The infrequent door-to-door solicitor usually gave up after one try.

Any thoughts of ignoring the doorbell ringer and going upstairs for that bubble bath were torpedoed when the bell rang again. And then again.

So much for her theory. "Okay, okay, I'm coming," Kate called out.

Cautiously, she opened it, the chain she'd hastily secured when she came in still in place. What she saw was a delivery boy standing there with what looked like half the local flower shop's supply of pink roses overflowing out of a large vase.

"Delivery for Ms. Manetti," the delivery boy told her before she had a chance to ask.

"Just a second." Shutting the door for a moment, Kate unlatched the chain and then reopened the door. As soon as she did, the flowers, all tucked carefully into a slender ivory pearl vase, were thrust into her hands. Stunned, Kate stared at them. No one sent her flowers.

"You're sure these are for me?" she questioned the delivery boy.

He held up his clipboard. "Your name and address matches," he said in a flat voice. "So I'm sure. Sign here, please," he instructed, thrusting the clipboard at her this time. Kate placed the vase down on the side table and quickly wrote her name in the space the delivery boy pointed to. "Thanks," he muttered, adding, "have-a-nice-day" as if it were all a single word to be carefully chewed before uttering.

Shutting the door with her back, Kate looked the vase over, searching for a card. And when she found it, she was no more enlightened than before. Maybe that wasn't quite accurate. It narrowed the playing field down to two.

The card said, "Thank you. J. Wainwright."

She frowned. They were both "J. Wainwright." Was Jonah thanking her for sharing a coffee with him, or was Jackson thanking her for whisking his brother away before he embarrassed both of them?

Closing her eyes, she offered up a quick, silent prayer. "Don't let it be from Jonah." The man might be tempted to follow up his delivery—and what was worse, it would mean that he knew where she lived. She liked having her privacy and *not* having a client turn up on her doorstep at will.

When what she was really hired for came to light, Jonah was not going to be happy. She wouldn't put it past him to camp out on her lawn in an effort to get her to reverse any new changes to the trust fund.

She glanced at the card that came with the flowers. Along with instructions on how to care for the roses was the name and phone number of the florist. First thing tomorrow, she promised herself, she would call and see if she could find out if that was *J* for Jonah or *J* for Jackson.

Until then, there was a bubble bath with her name on it, she thought, smiling to herself. And God, did she ever need it.

Stopping to smell the roses one last time, she went upstairs.

Chapter Six

The longer Kate remained in the bathtub, the harder it was for her to contemplate getting out. Periodically adding hot water to keep the temperature comfortable just increased her reluctance. But she had a feeling that if she didn't force herself to pull the plug and terminate this bath, she was in real danger of falling asleep and just possibly sliding down into the water.

Soaking in the tub had certainly done its job in relaxing her.

That evaporated the moment she thought she heard the doorbell ring again.

Kate had finally gotten out of the bathtub and was reaching for her bathrobe when she heard the doorbell chimes. Ordinarily, she wouldn't have. The radio or the music from her iPod would have blotted it out. Music was part of the winding-down process.

But tonight, because of everything going on in her head and the pace she'd put up with today, all she'd craved was a soothing silence. And because of the silence, she was able to hear someone ringing her doorbell.

Kate sighed. Who had declared her house the new Grand Central Station?

Quickly tugging on the ankle-length aqua-colored robe and knotting the belt at her waist, Kate flew down the carpeted stairs in bare feet.

The top half of her oversize front door was composed of colored beveled glass, which allowed her to make out the outline of the person standing on her front step.

A male person, she judged, given the breadth of the shoulders.

Another delivery? Somehow, she doubted it.

As she made her way to the door, Kate picked up her cell phone from the side table and dropped it into the right-hand pocket of her robe. Just in case she needed to make an emergency call. One of the lessons her father had inadvertently taught her was to be prepared for all contingencies.

Stopping short of the door, she raised her voice and called out, "Who is it?"

"Jackson."

Relieved that it wasn't Jonah popping up on her doorstep, Kate opened the door before she thought the situation through. Before the question, what was he doing here and how did he know where she lived, had a chance to take root.

For a fleeting moment, Kate felt vulnerable. But she banished that with her customary bravado.

"Party end sooner than you thought?" she asked wryly. She held the door open and stepped back so that he could come in.

Party ended the minute you left, Jackson caught himself thinking, but he wasn't about to admit it out loud for a whole host of reasons, the most important of which was not wanting his new family lawyer to think that there was no difference between him and Jonah. *He* was the civilized brother.

Although he wasn't feeling entirely civilized right now, not when he found himself staring at a woman wearing only a bathrobe and who was, more than likely, barefoot up to the neck under it.

The scent of jasmine and vanilla in the air didn't exactly help keep his mind on the straight and narrow.

Subtly taking in a breath, Jackson said, "No, it ended right on schedule. I just wanted to come and thank you in person."

So he did realize that she was running interference when she'd taken Jonah away, she thought, pleased. For a while there, she wasn't sure. But, being a lawyer had taught her to *never* assume anything without having it clearly delineated. So, adding just the right touch of innocence to her voice, Kate asked, "For?"

"For taking Jonah outside before he wound up causing a scene." His mouth curved in a humorless smile. "He has a tendency to get carried away without taking any of the consequences into consideration. I don't exactly relish being embarrassed, intentionally or not."

"Who does?" she countered quietly.

About to say something further, his line of vision drifted over to the vase with its two dozen plump, pink roses.

"Oh, they came." Jackson made no effort to hide the pleasure in his voice. "Nice to know you can still rely on some things."

She followed his gaze. The roses seemed to grow more gorgeous every time she looked at them. "You must have ordered them the second I walked out."

"I did."

She'd left the party just a little after six. That was late in the workday for florists. "I can't believe that you found someone to deliver them at a moment's notice at that time of the evening."

"You'd be surprised what you can get if you offer to pay triple the rate."

My God, she thought, considering the price of roses these days, that must have amounted to practically a small fortune.

"There was no need—" she began to protest.

"There was a need," he contradicted. He liked watching her in action, not to mention that he appreciated her handling Jonah. This was just his way of showing his gratitude.

Kate felt like baiting him just a little, although for the life of her, she wouldn't have been able to explain why.

"What if I was allergic to flowers?" Kate posed, amused.

"You're not."

Her amusement faded ever so slightly. More personal information. "How do you know that?"

"Same way I knew your address. I know things." The look on his face was unreadable. "I like to familiarize myself with the people I—um—" He realized that there was no really graceful way for him to conclude his statement.

"Hire," she supplied with a serene smile. "Don't worry, I'm not offended." What bothered her was that he'd investigated her, but in a way that was his right. And what made him a savvy businessman. "I am very secure in who and what I am. Lawyers are generally hired guns when it comes to corporate types." She looked at him pointedly.

He couldn't begin to visualize her as a "hired gun." However, just wearing boots and a hand-stitched leather holster...

He cleared his throat, stalling for a second as he reined himself in. What the hell was going on with him? "Even family lawyers?"

"Even family lawyers," she assured him, then explained. "In essence, you're hiring me to protect Jonah from himself even if he doesn't like the idea."

He was instantly alert. "You told him?"

"Not yet," she was quick to reassure him. "But when I do, he won't like it." It wasn't much of a guess. Jonah was locked into a heavy-duty romance with money and what it could do for him.

"I'll take care of that—telling him," Jackson clarified in case she wasn't following him. "You shouldn't have to be subjected to his first reaction to the news."

"I can take it, Jackson," she assured him with an amused smile. "I'm a big girl."

There's no disputing that. The top of her robe was parting a little with each breath she took. Jackson forced himself to look into her eyes.

"Did I interrupt something?" He nodded at her robe, still keeping his eyes on her face.

Kate had gotten so involved in the conversation, in having him here, she'd almost forgotten she was wearing next to nothing. She looked down at the robe and saw that it was parting. She tugged it back into place.

"Oh. No. I was just getting out of the tub when you rang the doorbell."

"Unwinding?" After dealing with Jonah for the first time, he could understand the need.

Her shoulders rose just a tad, then fell again. "Something like that."

"Jonah didn't try anything…?" He let his voice trail off.

"Jonah was fine," she quickly assured him, unconsciously placing her hand on his arm. "He was more than a little inebriated. We had coffee at that little shop on the corner and then I put him in a cab. He's going to have to get his car tomorrow," she added before he could bring that up.

"Wallace will get it for him."

The name was unfamiliar to her. "Wallace?"

"Wallace Brubaker. Jonah's all-around assistant. Wallace has been with him since Jonah was a teenager." Humor curved the corners of his mouth. "I'm not sure that Jonah could get dressed in the morning without Wallace."

Kate raised her eyebrows. "Maybe it's about time your brother learned a few basics like that," she suggested. "Might make him more in tune to the real world."

The scent of her bath salts was getting to him. Vanilla and jasmine. He assumed that they were clinging to her skin. Whatever the case, the combined scent was definitely getting under *his* skin. It was a struggle to keep focused when his mind kept drifting to far more stimulating subjects than his brother.

He needed her to get dressed.

"Speaking of which," he said, trying to keep his voice light, "maybe you'd like to do that, too?"

Puzzled, she asked, "Do what?"

"Get dressed," he said, tactfully looking away.

Which made her look down at her robe again. The belt had loosened again, allowing for more movement. Very specific movement. The robe was parting a lot lower than she would have ever intended on her own. One more careless shrug and it was all over.

"Oh." This time the single word was bursting with thinly veiled embarrassment. She tugged the belt tighter, bringing the two halves of the robe closer together. "Maybe I should get dressed," she agreed, attempting a segue.

Jackson nodded, deliberately keeping his eyes focused above her neck. "Good idea. I'll wait down here."

She wondered if he realized that he'd just invited himself to stay, or was he just accustomed to doing that without thought? Even so, she sensed a tension running through him. Somehow, she doubted that this time around the tension had anything to do with the subject of Jonah.

Stopping halfway up the stairs, Kate turned around, unable to resist asking, "Am I making you uncomfortable, Jackson?"

He came to the foot of the stairs and looked up. There was a small smile on his lips that she couldn't begin to fathom. "You have no idea," was all he said to her.

It was enough to warm her. And warn her. She was standing on very thin ice.

Taking a deep breath, Kate promised, "I'll be right back," and went up the rest of the stairs a lot more quickly.

Jackson tried not to notice the way the damp robe clung to her curves as she went.

But he couldn't help himself.

Kate couldn't remember when she'd gotten dressed so fast. The closest was the time she was in college and she'd woken up with only twenty minutes to get dressed and get to her constitutional law final. This time, she made it in less than five.

Part of her hurry was because she didn't want to keep Jackson waiting. And part of it was because some small part of her was afraid that Jackson might rethink the situation, and his gallantry, and decide to come up to "help" her get dressed.

The thought of being naked around the man had her fingers getting in each other's way as heat traveled up and down her body.

When she sailed down the stairs five minutes later, Kate was wearing jeans and a dark blue pullover, its sleeves pushed up on her arms to just below her biceps. She was still barefoot and her hair was secured in a ponytail. The only makeup she'd hastily applied was lipstick. She looked like a freshman in college and nothing like the young woman who had graduated in the top five percent of her class at Stanford.

Jackson was exactly where she'd left him, at the foot of the stairs. Except that he was facing the door rather than looking up.

He turned around when he heard her, about to comment that he'd never known any woman to get dressed as fast as she had, even during an earthquake. But the comment died the moment he looked up at her. A last-minute effort kept his jaw from dropping.

The woman who had come to his rescue at the party had been a gorgeous, sophisticated creature. The one he now stared at had a sweetness to her he hadn't glimpsed at first.

"Where's your big sister?" he asked.

Kate was aware of her appearance. As if she'd just

fallen off a turnip truck. But she wasn't trying to impress this man. She was just trying to be herself and this was how she looked when she wasn't being a lawyer.

"Very funny. Sometimes I like to be casual," she told him.

Maybe she liked being casual, but there was nothing casual about his reaction to her, Jackson thought.

The next moment he reminded himself that this was his lawyer. He wasn't supposed to react to her on anything but a professional level. A casual, teasing flirtation was one thing, but this was something else. Something that he hadn't felt in a very long time. Something that he really didn't welcome.

"Most women over the age of fifteen wouldn't venture out in public without any makeup," he observed.

Yet there she was, fresh-faced and beautiful. She made him nostalgic for simpler times. Times when all he had to concern himself with was his own life and the future was wide open. And the threat of unbelievably gut-wrenching pain was not even a remote reality.

"This isn't public," Kate pointed out. "It's private."

She realized that her words could easily be misconstrued. If it had been Jonah on the receiving end, she was fairly certain he'd attempt to make the most of "private" and she might have even been forced to fight him off right now.

She flushed and murmured, "You know what I mean."

Yes, he knew what she meant. Thank God one of them was grounded. Opening his jacket, Jackson took out the envelope he'd brought with him. The contents of the envelope—as well as wanting to personally thank her—was why he'd actually come here in the first place.

"Before I forget—" he handed the envelope to her "—I thought you might want this."

Accepting the manila envelope, she looked down at it. It was thick and bulky. Kate raised her eyes to his.

"The papers for the original trust fund I take it?" she guessed.

Jackson nodded. "The very same."

She appreciated the effort, but she hadn't wanted him to go out of his way. The man was undoubtedly tired.

"You didn't have to come over with them tonight," Kate told him. Tired, she was in no shape to go over legal papers.

Jackson waved a dismissive hand at her protest. "It was the least I could do after you distracted Jonah for me."

Kate smiled and lifted one slender shoulder in a shrug. "Oh, Jonah's not so bad," she told him.

While he appreciated the fact that she seemed to have identified the *real* Jonah, he needed her to understand that she still had to be careful around Jonah.

"Don't let him know you think that." Jackson was dead serious. He'd seen his older brother go through more than his share of women. Some had actually been decent. Others had been there strictly because of Jonah's money. All had made him accustomed to getting his way. "Otherwise, he'll be pledging his undying love to you within a week."

"Don't worry, that wasn't a personal observation, that was strictly from a lawyer's point of view," she told Jackson, then, to reassure him, she added. "I'm not about to get involved with him, either."

It was only after the word was out that Kate realized her slip. The look on Jackson's face when their eyes met told her that he'd caught it, as well.

"'Either'?" he questioned, his tone indicating interest.

Kate had always prided herself for being good at damage control. Now was no different. She rose to the occasion.

"Meaning I don't get involved with any of my clients, not in that way." This needed more explaining, she could tell. "I can be understanding. I can give you a shoulder to cry on, a hand to hold in trying times, a sympathetic ear to listen to your troubles." And then she delivered the most important part of her statement. "But all my other body parts are strictly mine and not for lending out."

He laughed then, amused, charmed and definitely intrigued. But then, if he was being honest with himself, he'd already been all of those things before he ever reached her doorstep. But he wasn't at liberty to enjoy any of those sensations—because he remembered the other side of the coin and he was not about to open himself up to that—ever again.

"I think I'm going to give your mother a finder's fee for bringing you to my attention." She seemed puzzled and Jackson went on to say, "I have a very strong feeling that this is going to be one hell of an association, Katherine."

The butterflies in her stomach that had suddenly and without warning risen up from their dormant state told her that she shared the same feeling.

In spades.

Which meant trouble.

Chapter Seven

"Can I offer you some coffee?" Kate asked, doing her best to sound nonchalant.

She had a sudden, urgent need to keep busy, to do something with her hands. This unsettling restlessness stirred up inside of her and she wasn't quite sure how to handle it. She hoped that if she just kept busy until it went away, she'd be all right.

Coffee's not what I'd like you to offer me.

The thought streaked across Jackson's mind without preamble, surprising him as much as he reasoned it would have surprised her, had he said the words out loud. But there was no way he could turn the thought into reality. Not with her.

Although he hadn't exactly been a monk, Rachel's death when he was in college had scarred him. The pain he'd gone through, losing her, wasn't something he wanted to endure again. The easiest way to avoid pain was to avoid a real relationship. Which is what he did.

If things looked as if they might, even remotely, be taking a serious turn, he broke it off. It was as simple as that.

And right now, he had the uneasy feeling that what hummed between him and Kate could very easily become serious if he allowed himself to give in to the very primal urges ricocheting inside his body.

Besides, having any personal relationship with this woman might, by its very existence, taint the nature of the trust fund he was trying to have resurrected. At the very least, it would make for a hell of a tabloid story, one Jonah would bring to the news media's attention in an effort to get what he felt was rightfully his.

But despite his resolve, Jackson still couldn't help wondering what Kate's body would feel like, pressed up against his. Not being able to scratch that itch just made him more aware of it.

The corners of Jackson's mouth quirked into a quick, enigmatic smile. "No, but thanks for the offer. I should be going," he explained. "I've already taken up too much of your time."

She didn't see it quite that way. He'd brought over the paperwork she'd requested. That in turn would help her get a jump start on Monday morning.

"Well, don't feel bad about that," she told him. "It's part of the package. You have me on retainer, remember?"

Her reasoning amused him. "Does that mean I was getting charged by the hour when you came by to the office tonight?"

"I haven't quite worked that out yet," Kate told him, an easy smile on her lips. "I was initially coming there for these papers," she pointed out, holding up the envelope he'd just given her. And then her smile reached her eyes. They crinkled. "Don't worry, Jackson. I'm not that mercenary. Consider coming to your party a freebie."

"And subtly drawing Jonah away?"

"More of the same," she answered.

"That would make you quite a bargain," he replied, only half kidding.

"So I've been told."

This time, the pull he felt between them was a little stronger. Jackson decided that he needed to leave before he found another excuse to stay—and did something he wasn't supposed to.

"Well, like I said, I'd better be going." But even as he repeated the trite phrase, reluctance to vacate the premises kept him in place. "Thanks again for getting Jonah to leave."

"Don't mention it." Taking the initiative, Kate turned toward the door, silently ushering him out. To seal the deal, she indicated the envelope and promised, "I'll get back to you on this." Because she knew that he probably wanted a tentative time frame, she added, "Most likely on Tuesday."

Jackson nodded. "Sounds good."

He lingered a split second longer by the door. He couldn't remember ever wanting to kiss a woman as much as he wanted to kiss her. Desperate for a way to label and contain this feeling, he told himself that it had to do with forbidden fruit. He knew he shouldn't kiss her so he wanted to. No big mystery there. He just had to continue resisting until the feeling passed.

"I'll see you soon," he told her.

Go already, she silently pleaded. She didn't know how much longer she could go on, ignoring the crackle of electricity between them. "Yes, you will."

She could feel her resolve cracking into tiny little pieces.

Damn it, Jackson, why aren't you kissing me? I was practically naked in front of you. Didn't that create some sort of reaction from you?

Maybe, instead of a warm bath, she should have just taken a cold shower. If this was Jonah instead of Jackson standing on her threshold, all she would have had to do was allow her glance to linger suggestively. Kate was fairly confident that by now, several sheets would have been incinerated from the heat of the lovemaking that would have ensued.

But she wasn't attracted to Jonah, she was attracted to Jackson. And she was going to pay. Big time. Unless she could do it on her terms.

"Good night," he murmured.

Jackson turned and began to walk away. She started to close the door. Suddenly, he doubled back and thrust his hand in the way, preventing her from completely shutting the door.

"Forget something?" Kate asked, keeping her voice mild even as she felt her heart leap up into her throat.

He needed to have his head examined. He'd almost been in the clear. "Kate…"

Her breath backed up in her lungs. "Yes?" she whispered between dry lips.

He'd started this, he needed to finish it—before she thought she was working for a village idiot. "How much would it complicate things if I kissed you right now?"

Outwardly, she strove for a semblance of calm. She could control this, she silently insisted. This was purely a physical thing, nothing more. "That all depends."

"On?" he prodded.

Just the slightest hint of a smile curved her lips. "On the way you kiss."

Very slowly and carefully, Jackson silently released the breath he'd been holding. "You want to find out?"

She lifted her chin. "I've never turned my back on a challenge."

"Good thing to know," he told her just before he slipped his arms around her and drew Kate closer to him. His mouth came down on hers.

At bottom, Kate would have said that she wasn't expecting the earth to move. Shimmy maybe, but not actually move.

She should have known better.

The kiss did not engulf her. Not at first. Warm, gentle, coaxing, it still managed to open a door to another world. Opened it until she suddenly found herself free-falling through space. There was no longer a threshold, no longer a house. No longer anything but flash and fire and heat—incredible, soul-singeing, all-consuming heat.

Kate gripped his shoulders in order to hang on, afraid of tumbling to the bottom of a five-mile abyss and smashing into a million pieces.

More afraid that the kiss would stop before she had her fill.

Pressing her body against his, she was both sorry that she had gotten dressed and greatly relieved that she had at the same time. Because if she were still in that robe, there wasn't a single doubt in her mind how this kiss would have ended. In her bed, burning up those aforementioned sheets.

The moment his mouth touched Kate's, Jackson realized that he'd known all along what this would be like. Known that this petite, intelligent, animated woman with the killer curves and midnight-black hair had the power to ignite a fire within him at first contact.

He just had to keep it in perspective, that's all. While he could satisfy his curiosity about kissing her, he knew that he definitely could not allow this to progress to its natural conclusion. That would be violating a host of rules, not a single one of which clearly came to mind at the present moment.

Jackson framed her face with his hands, deepening the kiss just one more inch, then terminating the entire experience, albeit reluctantly.

But it was a matter of survival. His.

His mouth tingled as he drew his head back. "I'll be waiting for your call," he told Kate, stepping away from her.

Turning, he quickly walked away—before baser instincts than he'd just displayed made him sweep her up in his arms and make love with her no matter *what* the consequences.

"Uh-huh."

It was the only sound Kate could produce at the moment.

Her strength barely lasted long enough for her to close the door behind his departing back. The second the door met the jamb, she slid down to the floor, her back against the frame, her limbs utterly liquefied. Possibly forever.

Who was *that masked man?*

Talk about a kick, Kate thought.

Wow. Oh wow.

It probably had something to do with her brain being fried, but she couldn't remember *ever* reacting to a man like this. Not even Matthew. He had turned her on, yes, but this was way beyond just physical attraction. Had her new client not left when he had, she would have been in dire danger of just ripping off his clothes and then launching an assault on him until he made love with her.

And wouldn't that *look lovely on your review? Get a grip, Kate. You know where this is going to wind up. And you're not going there again, understand?*

Using the doorknob for support, Kate slowly pulled herself up to her feet. She needed a stiff drink, she decided. Maybe several, so that she wasn't tempted to jump into her car and drive to Jackson's house to end what he had started.

When first Monday and then Tuesday came and went, enough time had passed for her to return to her senses. She was grateful that she hadn't gone with her urges. Something she'd regret.

But that didn't mean that the memory of the toe-curling kiss had faded or even degraded from an A-plus to a B-minus. The spectacular incident was still very much an A-plus, but she would have to be content with keeping it as a fiery memory. Under no circumstance could she allow herself to get carried away, not again. There were definitely times when the "road not taken" was best not taken. Especially when she knew where that road led.

Putting in a full day and then some on Monday and then Tuesday, she was in the office a full hour before she was supposed to be on Wednesday. She was more than two-thirds finished with the rough draft of what Jackson had asked her to do. After Matthew, work became her solution for everything.

This time, it was her way of handling all that charged, unfettered energy racing around inside of her.

In his office, continuing to familiarize himself with the particular, inner workings of this particular district of Republic National and its individual branches, Jackson frowned. He stared at the column of numbers on the Excel spreadsheet currently on his monitor. He'd just been conducting a random check on some of the accounts and he'd accidentally come across an inconsistency.

It was a shortfall, small in the scheme of things but definitely there.

He'd been following the thread now for the last three hours, pulling up screen after screen, the tension inside him growing. Each time he thought he'd just made a mistake, there was that little blip, that tiny grain of sand inside his shoe. In this case, it wasn't sand, it was missing funds. The bank's funds.

Someone was skimming.

Embezzling.

It was an ugly word, an uglier reality. And it had begun at precisely the same time as his transfer to this district had occurred.

Coincidence or deliberate?

At the moment, he couldn't trace the disappearing funds back to their source, but because of the glaring time line, he knew that it could be interpreted to make him look guilty as hell.

Who would set him up? Or was he just being paranoid about this?

Jackson scrubbed his hand over his face, trying to think, to sort out his scrambled thoughts. He definitely didn't need this. Dealing with his brother, who seemed to suspect something, and this attraction to Kate were bad enough. A possible embezzlement scandal was like the proverbial last straw.

Except that he couldn't allow it to break him.

Given that, what could he do? Was it one of the other bank officers, taking advantage of the confusion that his transfer had temporarily generated? After all, he was replacing a district manager, Alan Jefferies, who he'd heard, had to be "convinced" to take early retirement.

Convinced? Or coerced? And if the latter, why?

Or was the culprit one of the score of tellers this branch had, deftly removing funds in order to pay off a gambling debt? God knew he was more than passingly familiar with that kind of a situation, thanks to Jonah's latest addiction.

For all he knew, this might even be connected to Jonah in some fashion. He just didn't have enough information.

Biting off a curse, Jackson felt one hell of a headache coming on.

He didn't hear the phone on his desk ring at first. He was that consumed by what he was doing. But after the second time, the ringing registered. Even so, he fleetingly entertained the idea of just ignoring whoever it was on the other end of the line.

But he didn't have that luxury. Not as a district manager. Stifling several choice, terse words, Jackson yanked the receiver up from its cradle. As he put it against his ear, he barely refrained from snapping out his surname. "Wainwright."

"I have a rough draft of the papers drawn up," said the voice on the other end of the line.

Recognition was swiftly followed by a wave of warmth. Kate.

"So soon?" he asked, surprised. This was Wednesday morning. Despite her promise Friday night, he hadn't really expected to hear from her until at least the end of the week. He knew he wasn't her only client and he didn't think she'd drop everything to do his bidding. Moreover, there were still three weeks left until Jonah's birthday. They had time.

He heard her laugh.

"Hey," Kate said, "when you're good, you're good. Seriously, it turned out to be easier than I anticipated, thanks to Jonah's documented penchant for excess. He virtually made your case for you."

For a brief moment, Jackson thought he could detect a smile in her voice. He visualized one on her lips.

Though he tried not to let it, the image stirred him.

Jackson took a breath. He made a decision. He needed someone to talk to. Someone to brainstorm this problem with. The logical choice would have been one of the bank's lawyers, but he didn't know how far up the chain this embezzlement went, if it was embezzlement.

Despite all the hours he'd logged in at Republic National up north, down here he was essentially "the new guy." New guys had to tread lightly.

And as the new guy, he had only the ultimate clout that the others were willing to cede to him. In this precarious position, he really didn't want to make waves, or inadvertently have suspicion point to him. Especially not until he figured out who was stealing and just how much had been stolen.

"I need to see you," he told her without any kind of preamble.

"Are you asking me as the man who is retaining me, or as…?" She didn't finish, letting him fill in the line as her voice trailed off.

"Is there a third choice?"

"Not that I'm aware of, but I always like to leave myself open to things," she said with an amused laugh.

"I need a friend," he finally told her. She made no response to that. Not a good sign. Still, Jackson heard himself asking, "How soon do you think you can get here?"

If he was asking for the impossible, he might as well know now.

"I'm on my way right now," she told him. He thought he heard the sound of a drawer being closed on the other end. She was reaching for her purse, he guessed.

The next moment, he chastised himself that he was overreacting. This just wasn't like him.

"No," he ordered suddenly.

"I'm not on my way right now?" Kate questioned, puzzled.

"No," he repeated. "Don't come. I'm probably just making too much of this."

She had no idea what "this" was but she did note the consternation in his voice. That meant something was bothering him. Whether he actually needed a lawyer or a friend was moot. He needed her in whatever capacity he chose to place her in. That was good enough for her.

"You don't strike me as an alarmist," she told him. "So, unless there's a major accident involving farm animals on the freeway, I should be there in about twenty minutes."

Jackson tried again. "Look, forget what I said. I don't feel right about making you drop everything and just come running like this."

But he was stating his argument to the dial tone. Kate had already left the office.

Chapter Eight

Kate didn't arrive at his office in the promised twenty minutes. She arrived there in seventeen, slightly breathless because she had walked quickly from the underground parking facility where she'd left her car to the bank of elevators and then even more quickly down his hallway.

The moment he saw her, Jackson rose from his desk and crossed to her with his hand outstretched.

He was grateful she was there, but at the same time, he also felt guilty for making her come. Guilty as well as foolish. There was still the chance that he was making a mountain out of the proverbial mole hill.

But even if he wasn't, this was something he should

be able to handle on his own without outside emotional support.

"I take it there was no accident involving farm animals on the freeway," he said by way of a greeting, recalling the last thing she'd said to him before terminating their phone call.

"As luck would have it, no," she answered amiably.

Kate put down the briefcase she'd brought with her. The newly drawn up trust-fund papers were inside. For the time being, that was placed on the back burner. She parked the Italian leather briefcase next to his desk. Though he was trying to mask it, she could see that Jackson was agitated.

"Now, other than the usual, run-of-the-mill reason," Kate began warmly, "why do you feel that you need a friend?"

Several responses, all entrenched in small talk, rose to his lips, but they faded away. He owed her the truth. "I need to talk something out."

Kate gracefully dropped into the chair in front of his desk, making herself as comfortable as she could under the circumstances. She gave him her full attention. "So talk."

Jackson sat down in his chair, the rigid tension of his body in direct conflict with the small smile on his lips. The smile vanished the moment he spoke. "I think someone at the bank is embezzling."

Kate's eyes widened ever so slightly. The news surprised her. "Isn't that a rather difficult thing to do in this day and age?"

Get **2** Books **FREE!**

Silhouette® Books,
publisher of women's fiction,
presents

Silhouette®
SPECIAL EDITION

FREE BOOKS!   Use the reply card inside to get two free books!

FREE GIFTS!   You'll also get two exciting surprise gifts, absolutely free!

GET 2 BOOKS

We'd like to send you two *Silhouette Special Edition*®
novels absolutely free. Accepting them puts you under
no obligation to purchase any more books.

HOW TO GET YOUR
2 FREE BOOKS AND 2 FREE GIFTS

1. Return the reply card today, and we'll send you two *Silhouette
   Special Edition* novels, absolutely free! We'll even pay the postage!

2. Accepting free books places you under no obligation to buy
   anything, ever. Whatever you decide, the free books and gifts are
   yours to keep, free!

3. We hope that after receiving your free books you'll want to
   remain a subscriber, but the choice is yours—to continue
   or cancel, any time at all!

EXTRA BONUS

You'll also get two free mystery gifts! (worth about $10)

FREE!

Return this card promptly to get
2 FREE BOOKS and 2 FREE GIFTS!

SPECIAL EDITION

YES! Please send me 2 FREE *Silhouette Special Edition*® novels, and 2 free mystery gifts as well. I understand I am under no obligation to purchase anything, as explained on the back of this insert.

About how many NEW paperback fiction books have you purchased in the past 3 months?

❏ 0-2
EZWR

❏ 3-6
EZKS

❏ 7 or more
EZK4

235/335 SDL

FIRST NAME

LAST NAME

ADDRESS

APT.#

CITY

STATE/PROV.

ZIP/POSTAL CODE

Visit us at:
www.ReaderService.com

Offer limited to one per household and not valid to current subscribers of Silhouette Special Edition books. Please allow 4 to 6 weeks for delivery. Offer valid while quantities last. All orders subject to approval. **Your Privacy**—Silhouette Books is committed to protecting your privacy. Our Privacy Policy is available online at www.ReaderService.com or upon request from the Reader Service. From time to time we make our lists of customers available to reputable third parties who may have a product or service of interest to you. If you would prefer for us not to share your name and address, please check here ❏. **Help us get it right**—We strive for accurate, respectful and relevant communications. To clarify or modify your communication preferences, visit us at www.ReaderService.com/consumerchoice.

▶ DETACH AND MAIL CARD TODAY!

(S-SE-05/10)

If offer card is missing, write to The Reader Service, P.O. Box 1867, Buffalo, NY 14240-1867 or visit www.ReaderService.com

BUSINESS REPLY MAIL
FIRST-CLASS MAIL   PERMIT NO. 717   BUFFALO, NY

POSTAGE WILL BE PAID BY ADDRESSEE

THE READER SERVICE
PO BOX 1867
BUFFALO NY 14240-9952

NO POSTAGE
NECESSARY
IF MAILED
IN THE
UNITED STATES

There were security programs safeguarding the bank's depositors and investors. But this wasn't happening online.

"Sometimes the simplest approaches are the best. People expect this sort of thing to be done online, by clever hackers." He waved a hand at the screen on his desk. "There's no sign of anything like that going on."

"Then how do you know that funds are being embezzled?"

"Because there's a shortfall. A little here, a little there," he told her. "Someone is *physically* stealing small amounts at a time." He blew out a frustrated breath. "Whoever it is that's doing it is literally 'skimming' off the top."

This was the digital era. There was no such thing as privacy anymore. "Nothing show up on your surveillance cameras?"

He'd already thought of that. But this whole problem was still very fresh.

"I haven't started checking them yet," he admitted. "The moment I do, it'll give whoever's doing this a heads-up."

He had a point. If there *was* something going on. There was still a chance, albeit a small one, that it might all just be a miscalculation on his part.

"You're sure about this?" Kate pressed. "You *are* new to this position. It's possible that you might have made a basic mistake. You know, carried the hundreds column instead of the tens," she elaborated, only half kidding.

If he had to, he could add large strings of numbers in

his head. A unique feat in the day and age of heavy dependence on the computer and the scientific calculator.

"I've gone over everything five times," he told her. "The end-of-week figures don't tally. Each time, they're off by very little. But they *are* off."

Intrigued, she slid to the edge of her chair. "How much are you talking about?"

He didn't have to refer to his notes. It was all in his head. "At last total, almost ten thousand dollars. I know what you're thinking," he said before she could point the fact out. "That's not much money in the scheme of things. But it still puts the bank in the red by that sum."

He'd guessed wrong. That was definitely *not* what she was about to say. "It might not be much to you or the bank," Kate pointed out. "But it can be a fortune to someone who doesn't have it."

She could remember back when she was much younger, when money for Nikki and her mother was in scarce supply. She vividly remembered the concerned look on not only Maizie's face, but Nikki's, as well. Only people who had money could afford to be blasé about it.

"Okay," she recapped, "so far we've established that you have to check the surveillance camera footage. Have you tried running background checks on your employees?"

"All Republic National Bank employees have background checks done on them before they're hired."

But Kate shook her head. "*Recent* background checks," she emphasized.

As far as he knew, it was only done once. "What are you getting at?"

He was right, Kate thought. Ten thousand wasn't all that much—unless it meant the difference between life and death and there was a bookie or a loan shark involved. "Someone could suddenly be living beyond their means, or is held captive by the same malady as your brother: they're addicted to gambling, to the rush that comes from winning."

He never could understand that. The so-called rush from winning didn't begin to balance out the sick feeling in the pit of a person's stomach that losing huge sums of money had to have generated. Pitting himself against the "house," whatever the house might be, had never held any allure for him.

"I'd need to have the investigation done off the books," he told her.

Kate nodded. "That was my thinking."

He considered the matter for a moment. "That means I can't use the bank's investigators." He looked at her. "Would you know anyone to recommend? Maybe someone your firm uses?" he suggested hopefully.

Kate didn't have to think before answering. "Yes— and no," she answered.

"Come again?"

"I know someone you can use, but it isn't anyone af- filiated with my firm. To be honest," she told him, "I think you'd be better off with an entirely private investigator."

The reference brought back memories of far less

complicated days and made him smile. "You mean like Thomas Magnum or Sam Spade?" he asked, naming two popular fictional characters.

"Yes, except real—and female," she qualified.

Jackson looked at her a little uncertainly. "A woman private investigator?"

Some things still took time to change, she thought. This was one of those last frontiers. "Don't look so skeptical, Jackson. Women can ask questions that men can't, and people just chalk it off to idle curiosity, nothing more."

That made sense, he supposed. He didn't care if the investigator was male or female, just thorough—and good. "I want this investigation to be kept strictly confidential. Is this someone you can vouch for?"

That was an easy one to answer. She grinned. "Absolutely. We grew up together. I have complete faith in her. If there's a secret life being led, Jewel is the one to find it for you. If she can't, there's nothing to be found," she assured him with feeling. "I'll give her a call and if she's free, I can bring her around tomorrow."

Now that he'd decided on a course of action, Jackson was anxious to get started. "This afternoon would be better. I want this resolved as quickly as possible."

She didn't blame him. "No one wants this kind of thing to linger," she agreed.

Opening her purse, she took out Jewel's business card. She knew Jewel's personal cell number by heart—

God knew she called it often enough. But Jewel's business phone was another matter. She'd never had to make use of it. Before now.

After tapping out the numbers on her cell-phone keypad, Kate listened to the phone on the other end ring. And ring. Finally, the voice-mail feature kicked in.

A melodic voice told her, "You've reached Parnell Investigations. Sorry, I'm on a case and can't answer your call. Leave your name and number after the beep and I'll get back to you as soon as possible."

Kate waited for the appropriate signal before saying, "Jewel, it's Kate. I've drummed up some business for you. One of my clients has need of your very particular set of talents as soon as possible. Call me when you get this." She snapped the phone closed and dropped it back into her purse. "I'll put her in touch with you the minute she calls," she promised.

That out of the way, Kate took a breath. "Now, do you want to review the papers extending the terms of Jonah's trust fund?" she asked. "I haven't filed the final paperwork yet, but that should just be a simple formality. I just wanted to review things with you in case you've had a change of heart."

"Why would I have a change of heart?" Jackson questioned.

She'd always believed that anything was possible. That was why God had created optimists. "Maybe Jonah suddenly had a life-altering experience and is now capable of being master of his own destiny," she suggested. Admittedly, the suggestion was more tongue-in-cheek than anything else.

"If that *ever* even remotely happened, I'd be calling up your mother to throw another party. A huge one," he emphasized. "No, from where I stand, I'm afraid that is never going to happen."

Meeting Jonah had allowed her to form her own opinion of the man. He'd struck her as harmless, but, unlike his brother, rather shallow. Kate tried to imagine what that had to be like, dealing with someone like Jonah on a regular basis. It must have been very trying for Jackson.

"I guess it's kind of like constantly dealing with Peter Pan," Kate speculated, raising her eyes to his to see if her comparison struck him as being on target.

"Yeah, except that Peter Pan's actions never threatened to bankrupt Tinker Bell or the Lost Boys," Jackson commented.

Kate knew he was serious, but she couldn't help being amused by the reference.

"Good point." Leaning over, she drew the briefcase closer to her and snapped the locks open, then took out the papers that were intended for Jackson's in-depth perusal. "Here." She pushed the pages into Jackson's hands.

Jackson quickly skimmed through the packet, occasionally pausing to reread something. From start to finish, it took Jackson all of five minutes.

Kate watched him, impressed. It had taken longer to

gather the papers together than for him to review them.
"Let me guess, you're a speed reader."

Jackson nodded. "In the interests of not being
buried under huge stacks of paperwork, I took a
course," he admitted.

If she'd read that fast, not a word of it would have
stuck. "And you retain everything?" she asked Jackson
skeptically.

He had the kind of mind that could call things up at
will. Whether it was a face or a passage, he only needed
to see it once and it was forever a part of him.

"If you have your doubts, you could quiz me," he
offered with a hint of a smile.

The questions she wanted to pose had nothing to do
with his skill or any legally binding statements. Her
questions would have been far more intimate in nature.

You're slipping again, she chided herself. *You
remember what'll happen if you do. Right now, he
doesn't seem to have any flaws, but he will. Disappointment's just right around the corner.*

Her mouth quirking in a fast smile, she dismissed the
offer.

"Maybe sometime when we both have nothing else
getting in the way," she told him. She could see by his
expression that he thought that an odd choice of words.
That made two of them. But the undercurrent of electricity that was, even now, humming between them
would *definitely* get in the way.

She glanced at the packet on the desk before him.

This was what she had to focus on, nothing else. "So, is it satisfactory?"

It was hard to drag his mind back on the topic. Her perfume swirled around him, causing his thoughts to drift toward things that had nothing to do with his work. It took effort to bank down the grin that the images running through his head coaxed to the foreground.

Taking a breath, he nodded at the papers. He had to remember that this was important. Jonah's future depended on it. "Looks great. You're sure that it'll hold up in court?"

She wondered if nerves had prompted him to ask, or if he actually thought that she was capable of doing a slapdash job. "Yes, I'm sure it'll hold up. You're thinking that Jonah's going to contest it?"

If he were a betting man—and he wasn't—this was what was known as a sure thing.

"Damn straight. The last two weeks Jonah's gone out of his way to let me know how much he's really counting on this money. My guess is that he's got most of it, if not all of it, already accounted for and, most likely, spent." This despite the fact that the trust fund came to a considerable amount.

Jackson was instinctively bracing himself for the outraged assault, alternating with expressions of genuine hurt, all of which would come to pass within a few minutes of Jonah's learning that the original trust fund was being resurrected. This despite the fact that, at bottom, his brother had to know that this was all being done with only his best intentions and welfare in mind.

Since Jackson had just given his approval, she needed to move on to the next step.

Kate rose to her feet, tucking the papers back into her briefcase. There was still enough time to get down to Civic Center Drive where the courthouse was located.

"All right," she said pleasantly, "if there isn't anything you want to change or add, I'll go down to the courthouse to file this. In the meantime, I'll be waiting for Jewel's call. I'll let you know the minute I hear from her."

Jackson nodded, telling himself that looking forward to her phone call shouldn't be at the top of his list of priorities. But even a man completely dedicated to his career had to look forward to something outside the box.

"Fair enough."

Kate began to leave, then stopped. She put her own interpretation to the expression on his face. "Don't worry, Jackson," she assured him. "We'll get whoever's behind all this." Even if Jewel wasn't her friend, she wouldn't have felt any hesitation in assuring him, "Jewel *is* very good at ferreting things out."

He had no doubt of this. Unfortunately, he couldn't offer her the same courtesy. He had a feeling that she might not appreciate the fact that, for one fleeting second, he'd let his mind indulge in a torrid fantasy of her.

"I was just thinking about Jonah," he told her. As he spoke, he switched gears. The rest was easy, because his mind *had* gone in this direction earlier. "Wishing things were different."

This had to be really difficult for Jackson, Kate thought. She knew how she'd feel if there was a schism between Kullen and her. Hurt, devastated and angry. She'd come out of her corner swinging, furious that he would allow something as cold as money come between them.

"Maybe he'll surprise you and still come around," she said encouragingly. "Your brother could be one of those late bloomers. You know the type. Just as you give up on them, they suddenly become mature and responsible in the second half of their lives."

Even though he desperately wanted that to be true, Jackson knew better.

There was a smile in his eyes as he asked, "And do you believe in the Easter Bunny, too?"

There wasn't a second's hesitation on her part. "With all my heart," she told him with the kind of conviction that swayed juries and convinced reluctant participants in civil suits to come around.

Her enthusiasm gave him an iota of hope. The light in her eyes warmed him.

He asked before he could think better of it. "Kate, are you busy tonight?"

When she wasn't in the office burning midnight oil, her evenings were pretty solitary these days. But evenings at home were few and far between. "Well, I'm going to be trying to get hold of Jewel again once I file these papers."

Damn it, why was her pulse jumping around so much. He wasn't asking her out. And even if he did, she really couldn't accept. Lines would wind up getting blurred.

Would? she mocked herself.

Out loud, Kate asked, "Why? What did you have in mind?"

He watched her face as he told her, "Dinner."

"Dinner's always good," she said noncommittally, her mind racing, drawing up a chart of pros and cons. She tried to add weight to the pros even as she knew she should be doing it to the opposite side.

His eyes on hers, Jackson half asked, half suggested, "Have it with me?"

"A working dinner?" It was a straw, but she grasped it. Inclining her head after what was supposed to appear to be a debate, she said, "Sure, why not?"

He didn't want to talk business tonight, at least, he didn't want to *plan* to talk business tonight. "I was thinking more along the lines of—"

Kate cut him short. In order to alleviate her conscience, she had to put the situation in a certain light. "A working dinner." It wasn't a question, it was a statement.

He knew better than to press the point. She'd obviously worded it the way she had for a reason. Whatever it took to get some time alone with her, he was on board.

"A working dinner it is," he echoed. "I'll pick you up—"

Again she contradicted him. "I'll meet you there," she told him. It would be safer that way, less tempting for her to go home with him and *really* sample those lips she'd been looking at so intently.

"We'll meet at the restaurant," he agreed without missing a beat. Then his curiosity got the better of him. "Any particular reason it has to be that way?"

"You're a new client," she reminded him. "Appearances are important."

He wasn't all that into appearances, but he could understand how she might be. Was she worried about the way things looked to the senior members of the firm she worked for, or was she concerned about the way the people who worked for him would perceive things?

"I suppose you're right. Would you like to know which restaurant?" he asked, amused.

"Might make it easier," she allowed, a smile shining in her eyes.

He mentioned the name of a restaurant that prided itself on its variety of meat and potatoes dishes, Swift's. It had been around since way before he'd moved up to San Francisco. In his estimation, it might be interesting to find out if the food there was still as good as he remembered.

"Swift's," she repeated, nodding. Again, she lingered. "And you know, my offer still stands."

He found the reference a little unclear. "What offer's that?"

"I can review the key points of the new trust fund with Jonah." There was a reason for her suggestions. "He might not rage at a woman."

Jackson laughed shortly. "No, ordinarily he wouldn't.

However, since you're also the lawyer who put all this in motion, he just might make an exception."

She wasn't intimidated. She'd been in the middle of battles between outraged family members and survived. "Still, if you find it hard to tell him, that's what I'm here for."

Oh, he could think of a lot of other uses for her that had nothing to do with sensitive older brothers who felt betrayed.

Rousing himself, Jackson said, "I'll see you at six. Unless you hear from your friend earlier."

She nodded. "Six," she repeated, then echoed, "Unless I hear from Jewel."

And with that, Kate forced herself to cross the threshold and finally leave—before she came up with another reason to stay.

Chapter Nine

"If this is a working dinner, exactly what is it that you think you're working?"

The question was directed from Kate to Kate, or at least to the image she saw reflected in her wardrobe door mirror.

The bed behind her looked as if it was sagging under the growing weight of clothes in her hunt for the perfect outfit. So far, she'd found fault with each one she'd tried on.

What she was currently reviewing with a super-critical eye would have never found its way into the work place—unless "work" involved squiring upscale clients who had a large wad of disposable cash to waste by investing it in a single evening's "entertainment." High priced, but still a lady of the evening.

"You don't want Wainwright getting the wrong idea," she told the reflection sternly as she began to snake the outfit she had on down her hips. When it hit the floor, she picked it up and flung the garment onto the pile accumulating on the bed.

Standing in sky-blue lingerie, Kate frowned. At this rate, she would either have to cancel dinner, falling back on the age-old cliché that she had nothing to wear, or she would resort to something her mother used to refer to as a "party dress." The term dated back to when she was eight years old.

"Of course, you could always wrap yourself up in cellophane," she quipped. "Or go naked."

Her palms were damp, she realized. This was ridiculous.

Why was she so nervous? Kate upbraided herself. This wasn't a date, this was just a meeting with a client that happened to take place over cutlery and selected cuts of beef, nothing more. That he happened to be gorgeous, well, that wasn't her fault. That was just an extraneous fact.

Determined to regroup, Kate sank down onto the only tiny corner of her queen-size bed that wasn't littered with discarded clothing.

She knew damn well what was at the bottom of all this. While professionally she had a sharp legal mind coupled with keen instincts, the instincts she had in her private life left a little to be desired.

Who was she kidding? They left a great deal to be desired. A great deal, she emphasized. The same woman who could succinctly read a jury, an opposing counsel and the most poker-faced of judges suddenly had the in-depth instincts of a pet rock when it came to reading a man in her private life. And she had the scars to prove it.

That was the only explanation for not picking up any of Matt's warning signs. Matthew McBain, a dashing, top-flight criminal lawyer who had single-handedly turned sleeping around into an art form. There'd been whispers about his extracurricular activities and, though it hadn't been easy for him, Kullen had come right out and told her what Matt was up to. But she, Pearl Pure-heart, had refused to believe it.

Until the evidence became so overwhelming and damning that only a first-class fool would have denied it. Her heart all but constricting in her chest, she gave in to the inevitable and had handed Matt his walking papers. Rumor had it that he'd found another warm bed before the day was out.

Matt always had a way of bouncing back, she thought cynically. While she didn't bounce so well. After Matt, she had finally admitted that her penchant for picking good-looking scoundrels had to go. The only way she could do that was to turn her back on dating.

It had been a very long time since she'd entertained the idea of socializing. Pretending to be tough as nails and utterly invulnerable, Kate might have fooled others, but, bravado aside, she couldn't fool herself.

And right now, despite everything she vowed to the contrary about this being a professional meeting over dinner, she was scared. Scared of being a fool again. Of leading with something other than her brain and suffering the consequences for it.

Why was she doing this to herself? she silently demanded of the image in the mirror.

"You're not entering a relationship, you're entering a restaurant to have dinner, that's it. End of story," she said out loud, underscoring her agitation. "You're the one making a big deal out of it. Nobody else is even noticing. Now get dressed and get the hell out of here," she ordered tersely.

The woman in the mirror didn't look convinced.

With a sigh, Kate shifted so that she could review—for a second time—the haphazard piles of clothing on the bed. Hopefully, she could find something halfway suitable that didn't require an intimate rendezvous with an iron, something she was less than apt at wielding.

Just as Kate located an outfit that, upon closer re-evaluation, she decided merited a passing grade, she heard her cell phone ring. The sound came from somewhere on the bed—muffled because it was obviously buried beneath layers of fabric.

"Oh God," she muttered. Kate began to toss clothes onto the floor in an effort to find the phone before it stopped ringing.

Maybe it was Jackson, calling to cancel. That would probably be for the best, she told herself. There was no chance of making a tactical error at dinner if there was no dinner.

But even as she pretended that she welcomed this possible turn of events, she felt the tips of each of her fingers turning cold.

There was just no winning.

Just as the song that comprised her ringtone ended, she finally located the phone. Flipping it open, she cried, "Hello, Jackson?" without bothering to glance at the name currently highlighted within the caller-ID screen.

"No, it's Jewel," the melodic voice on the other end of the call said. Her next words carried more than a little interest in them as she asked, "Who's this Jackson?"

"A client." Well, that was the truth, Kate silently said.

"A client, huh?" She knew that tone. Kate grimaced as she reacted to the probing sound. "What else is he, Kate?"

She was in no mood to be probed, even by one of her two best friends. Her guard automatically went up. "What do you mean?" she asked warily.

She could hear the smile in Jewel's voice. "Just that I can't seem to recall you ever being breathless about a 'client' before."

"I was just trying to locate my cell phone before you hung up. It was buried in a pile of—" No, she thought, mentioning the clothes would be a huge mistake. "Never mind." She dismissed the subject. "I'm glad you called me."

"So am I," she said heartily. The next words out of

her mouth told Kate that she wasn't about to back away. "Spill it, Kate."

"Spill what?" she asked, trying to sound innocent. Even to her own ear, it sounded forced. The vote was in. If she'd opted to be an actress when it came time to choose a career, she would have starved to death.

"Come off it, Kate," Jewel told her. "I make my living tailing unfaithful spouses. I've got keen powers of observation—and I know when someone's lying."

"Well, I think you and your 'keen powers of observation' need a little tune-up because you're definitely misfiring." She steered the conversation in another direction. "Anyway, I called you for a reason. I've got a client who needs some discreet investigating done."

Jewel sighed, weary. "Male or female?"

Kate thought of the people she'd seen at Jackson's party. She assumed he would want all of them looked into. "Both."

"Both?" Jewel repeated incredulously. "I think you just lost me." She tried her hand at filling in the blanks. "Your client's married and swings the other way, too?"

In a moment of sudden clarity, Kate went from being confused to realizing what Jewel had to be thinking. "No!" she cried sharply. "He doesn't want to have a spouse tailed. He doesn't have a spouse."

Since most of her surveillance work involved cheating spouses, Jewel was puzzled. "He doesn't?"

"No. He wants to have his tellers' recent dealings looked into." The silence on the other end told Kate that she needed to start at the beginning. "He's a district manager at Republic National Bank and he wants to make sure that no one in one of the branches he oversees has anything out of the ordinary going on." And then she illustrated what she meant. "Large deposits out of the blue, sudden lavish spending sprees, things like that." And then she cinched the deal. She put it in the form of a challenge. Jewel was every bit as competitive as she was. "Are you up to it?"

"An honest-to-goodness investigation that doesn't involve using a telephoto lens to take pictures of sweaty people stealing an hour's worth of passion in a seedy motel? Up to it? Kate, I think I'm going to cry."

Kate laughed. Jewel always had a flair for the dramatic. "I take it that means that you're available?"

"You bet I am," Jewel answered with enthusiasm. "Even if I wasn't available I'd be available. This'll be a breath of fresh air compared to what I've been doing." She savored the thought for half a beat before getting down to the pertinent questions. "What, where, when, who and how?"

"My client can answer the questions better than I can. I'll put you in touch with him," she promised before giving Jewel some of the more basic information. "His name's Jackson Wainwright—"

"Jackson Wainwright." Jewel rolled the name off her tongue, as if sampling it for familiar tastes. "Didn't I just read something in the local paper about him getting into it with a cop over creating a disturbance in public?"

"That's his brother Jonah and a whole other story. Jackson's the good brother. He just transferred down here from the bank's home office in San Francisco to keep tabs on his big brother before Jonah winds up hurting himself—and possibly someone else to boot."

"And where does investigating his employees come in?" Jewel asked. "Or does he want me to keep tabs on his brother, too?"

"No. Wainwright thinks someone's embezzling from one of his branches. He needs his employees' files reviewed, cross-referenced and all that good stuff you know how to do so well."

"Flattery will get you everywhere—and even if it didn't, taking on something new made your argument for you. Tell Wainwright that when I meet with him, I'd like him to give me a list of all the employees' names and social security numbers. That way I can get started right away."

"Sounds good to me," Kate told her. "So when can I set up a meeting? I think he's really anxious to get this thing started."

Jewel didn't even have to think about it. "Anytime he's free. My schedule's flexible. This less-than-sterling husband I've been tailing has already given me enough material to allow his wife to take him to the cleaners twice over. The guy's involved in a threesome even as we speak. I can have this all wrapped up by tonight."

Kate heard her friend sigh again, a little more deeply this time. She knew exactly what Jewel was thinking.

That this kind of thing, being paid to spy on cheating spouses, was beneath her. Jewel only took on these assignments to pay the bills while she waited for something better to come along. Who knew? Maybe this would somehow lead to her doing something else, something more interesting, more challenging and most important of all, something that didn't have her coming home wanting to take two showers to wash the stench of infidelity off her skin.

"Wonderful," Kate declared, knowing that if anyone could get information, it was Jewel. She was tenacious and, just as important, she had access to all sorts of people who could help her. "I'll let Wainwright know at dinner tonight."

The moment the words were out, Kate knew she'd slipped up.

"Dinner, huh?" The two words burst at the seams with all sorts of implications.

"It's a working dinner," Kate was quick to emphasize. But the damage, she knew, was done.

"Uh-huh."

"No, really," Kate insisted. She wanted Jewel to believe her. "I'm reworking the terms of a trust fund for his brother. It's about to expire and Wainwright thought that—"

"You don't have to explain to me, Kate," Jewel assured her. "I'm already in your corner. I'm your friend, remember?"

"And if you want to stay that way and know what's

good for you, you'll find a way to get rid of that smug, I-can-see-through-you tone in your voice."

"Yes, ma'am," Jewel teased. "Consider it done." She heard Jewel laugh, then clear her throat in a futile attempt to cover up the sound. "Call me as soon as you have a date."

The request took Kate completely by surprise. "What?"

"For me to meet Wainwright," Jewel clarified. And then she couldn't resist asking, "Why? What did you think I meant?" she pressed innocently.

Kate glanced at her watch. Oh God, she was going to be late. She was never late. Larger butterflies replaced the mid-size ones already circling in her stomach.

"I've got to go," she announced just before she flipped her phone closed. She had exactly five minutes to find something suitable to wear. Or cancel.

"You look terrific," Jackson said with unabashed appreciation, rising in his chair as the server brought Kate over to his table. He'd begun to think that she had changed her mind at the last minute and opted out. The wait, he now thought as his eyes swept over her, had been well worth it. She wore one of those little black dresses and it accentuated all the right places. His new family lawyer had quite a figure on her.

The compliment made her cheeks warm. She was grateful that the lighting was dim. "Thank you. I was running late so I really didn't get a chance to be very selective. This is just something I grabbed out of the closet and threw on."

He doubted the process had been that hurried. She looked far too good for that. But he saw no reason not to play along. "Haste looks good on you," he told her. "You should do it more often."

Something in his voice tipped her off. Kate's eyes narrowed as she studied his face. "You know I'm lying, don't you?"

"Lying's a bit harsh," he observed. And then he grinned. "But no woman I have ever known just 'throws' clothes on. Young or old, appearance matters to them. Although, I have to admit, if anyone could get away with the rushed, I-don't-give-a-damn look, it's you."

Kate toyed with the edges of her menu. "Thank you—I think."

"It was meant as a compliment," Jackson assured her. And then he sat back in his seat. "So, do you want to order first, or would you rather show me something you have tucked away in your clutch purse that'll qualify this as a 'working' dinner and make you feel better about being here like this?"

Ordinarily, she would have taken offense. But he'd said it so guilelessly that she found herself charmed instead.

"I don't have anything to show you," she admitted. "But I can tell you something instead."

"Okay," he said gamely, resting his hands on the edge of his side of the table. "What?"

"Jewel got back to me." There was no sign of recognition on Jackson's face when she said the name. "My friend who's a private investigator," she clarified.

"Oh, right," he said, remembering. "When can she meet with me?"

"She would be able to clear some time for you this coming Monday in the afternoon if that works for you."

Taking out his smartphone, Jackson opened it and consulted the feature that kept track of his schedule. It was one of the state of the art models that surrendered its information at a touch. He still had to flip through several screens before he found what he was looking for.

Nodding to himself, he flipped the phone closed and returned it to his jacket pocket. "Monday afternoon works out fine for me." He raised his eyes to her. "Say around two?"

"Two," she repeated with a nod. "I'll let Jewel know."

"All right," Jackson said with a nod. "Now that that piece of business is out of the way and we can officially refer to this as a 'working dinner,' what would you like to have for the eating portion of this dinner?" he asked her as he opened his menu.

You, on a plate, garnished with parsley.

Stunned, Kate blinked. The thought had come out of nowhere, ambushing her. Maybe it *had* been too long between men.

Better yet, she decided the next moment, she needed to get back to the gym again. If she exercised for an hour after a full day at work, she would definitely be too tired for these kinds of thoughts. And as an added bonus, if she followed this course of action, she mused, her body would be toned, as well.

Kate slanted a glance at her client. One perfectly shaped eyebrow arched. Clearly, Jackson was waiting for her to make her selection.

"How's the prime rib here?" she asked, glancing at the menu's second page.

"Excellent. Actually, to the best of my recollection, you can't go wrong ordering anything here."

That was good enough for her. Kate closed her menu and placed it on the outer edge of the table. "Then I guess I've made my choice. I like my meat rare."

Their eyes met and held for a moment. The smile on his lips told her that he took her words to mean something else entirely.

Maybe, subconsciously they did, she thought as her icy fingertips made an encore appearance. Right now, she was relieved that Jackson didn't have a reason to take hold of her hand.

Very subtly, she dropped one hand to her lap and then moved it ever so slowly until it was beneath her thigh. She had to warm her hands up somehow and aside from rubbing them against each other as if she meant to start a fire by magic, this was the only way.

Unless she got something hot to wrap her hands around to warm them.

She saw the server approach, ready to take their orders. "Ready to order?" the young woman asked.

"Coffee," Kate declared. "Could you bring me some coffee, please? Oh, and I'd like the prime-rib dinner." She went on to describe the way she wanted it prepared.

When she finished, Jackson repeated, "Coffee?" Usually that was ordered after the meal, not before. "Planning on pulling an all-nighter?" he asked.

She didn't need coffee for that, she thought, casting another glance in his direction. She was already way past being wired enough to remain up all night.

But she couldn't just leave his question hanging there, so she murmured, "You never know."

Chapter Ten

The meal was every bit as good as it had promised to be, more than living up to the restaurant's five-star reputation. The only thing that was better, in Kate's estimation, was the conversation.

When the server returned to clear away their dishes and ask about their choice for dessert, Kate shook her head. "I'd have to wear it, not eat it," she told the young woman.

The latter's eyes shifted to Jackson. "I'm pretty full, too," he told the server, then took a second glance at the back of the menu. The description he was reading more than sold itself. "Although this ice-cream dish sounds really good." Putting down the menu, he appealed to Kate. "Split it with me?"

The mere thought of eating another bite of anything almost made her sides ache. "I really don't think there's any room left in my stomach for even a breath, much less any kind of food."

"There's always room for ice cream," Jackson assured her cheerfully.

"I think you have your commercials mixed-up. That's Jell-O," she told him."

Jackson stood his ground. "Ice cream melts, Jell-O doesn't, at least not as quickly." He leaned over and took her hand in his. "C'mon, Kate," he coaxed. "Be adventurous."

She raised a skeptical eyebrow. "You consider eating ice cream adventurous?"

"In your case, yes," he teased. "You've got to start someplace."

Kate sighed, pushing the menu toward the server. Capitulating, she gave Jackson her terms. "All right, but you eat most of it."

"That's not really the idea behind 'splitting,' but all right." He looked at the server. "One order of Brandy Snowdrift and two spoons."

The woman nodded, tucked the menus under her arm, piled one empty plate on the other, then picked them up and gracefully withdrew.

"She'd better come back quick," Kate commented. "I can feel the food expanding in my stomach, taking up the last of any available space." Humor glinted in her eyes.

He liked talking to her. Liked enjoying simple

things with her. "You don't generally eat dinner, do you?" he guessed.

A good deal of the time, she couldn't get to the gym, or even have time for a brisk walk. She watched her weight by regarding food as fuel, not falling into the trap of thinking of it as a support system.

"My quota's usually about two meals, broken up and scattered throughout the day."

She had a very nice shape, but "really thin" was only a whisper away. "If you weighed any less, you'd prob-ably have to carry rocks in your pockets when our winds kick up around here." The Santa Anas could be fierce at times, pushing SUVs from one lane to another, up-rooting trees. How did someone as slender as Kate manage in weather like that?

A moment later, Jackson caught a movement out of the corner of his eye. Turning, he saw the server return-ing to their table. "Ah, it seems that if you wish for it, it will come," he told Kate.

Kate was about to ask him what he was talking about when the server unobtrusively placed a small pearl-white dish on the table. It was piled high with brandy-soaked French Vanilla ice cream, sumptuously smothered with whipped cream.

Kate's blue eyes widened. "I don't care how much this slides down, it's all got to pool together somewhere."

"I'll take the first spoonful," Jackson volunteered, adding, "It's a dirty job, but someone's got to do it." Slipping the spoonful between his lips, he closed his eyes for a moment, *really* enjoying the taste. Opening his eyes again, he told her, "This is even better than their prime rib."

As far as she was concerned, the two appealed to completely different taste buds. "I find that hard to believe."

"Okay, Doubting Thomasina." Jackson inserted the spoon into the mountain of ice cream, filling it. "See for yourself."

Holding the ice cream laden spoon aloft, he coaxed it to her lips.

The protest that she could feed herself faded away. A surge of heat made its appearance, encompassing her body. After a second, she opened her lips and let Jackson slip the spoon in.

Was it just her, or did that feel insanely sensual? Like something hot and yet cool at the same time had slid up and down her spine.

Was sliding up and down her spine.

"More?" he asked in possibly the sexiest voice she'd ever heard. Her heart was hammering practically loud enough to drown him out.

"More," she murmured, nodding.

Jackson fed her another spoonful, then brought one more to his own lips, his eyes never leaving hers. The temperature in the restaurant went up at least another fifteen degrees.

Possibly more.

She wasn't completely aware of things after that. What seemed like a huge bubble slipped over the two of them, sealing off everything beyond the table. Leaving just the two of them, one slowly depleting dish of ice cream and a single spoon doing double duty.

There was something hopelessly sexy about sharing not just the same desert, but the same spoon, Kate couldn't help thinking. Her entire body tingled with each spoonful.

By the time the ice cream was gone, so was she. Or at least it felt that way.

The server returned then and asked something that sounded like, "Would there be anything more?"

God, he hoped so, Jackson thought. Deceptively simple to the casual eye, the act of eating this ice cream with Kate had electrified him.

The server continued waiting for instructions. Jackson shook his head and handed her his credit card, all without looking away from Kate's face. The moment he heard the server retreat, he asked, "Would you like to come over for a nightcap?"

Her head was already spinning, and that had to be from the residual brandy vapors. While she knew how to handle her liquor, just this once, she wasn't going to take a chance. Someone had changed the ground rules on her when she wasn't looking.

"Right now, for whatever reason, I seem to be intoxicated. I don't think I should have anything more potent than what I've just had."

The beverage didn't matter. The company did. "Coffee, then," he suggested quietly. "Orange juice, diet soda. Whatever quenches your thirst."

It wasn't any of the above that would quench her thirst, Kate thought. It would be the man who was offering them.

Not a good idea.

This was where she begged off, saying something witty—or at the very least, coherent—as she turned him down. "All right," wasn't part of a refusal, and yet, those were the only words that found their way to her all but parched lips.

The server returned with the credit-card receipt. Jackson quickly signed it, then dug into his pocket and placed a large bill on top of the signed receipt. It was the woman's tip, one she wouldn't have to wait around until the slips were cashed at the end of the day—or longer.

"Wow," the girl exclaimed, picking up the bill. All pretense at being poised dropped instantly. "Thanks, mister."

In his position, he didn't get to see the effects a little more money had on people's lives.

"Don't mention it," he told her with a genial smile.

Was this for her benefit, or was he actually this generous? Kate couldn't help wondering.

"Do you always toss money at people?" she asked him once the woman had left.

"Only when the service is good."

Rising, Jackson came around behind her chair and helped her on with her lacey shawl. His fingers skimmed her bare shoulders, whether by accident or design, Kate didn't know. Either way, she was certain that the result would have been the same: giant butterflies dive-bombing into each other as the temperature of her skin rose again.

The cool night breeze hit her the moment they walked out. It was more than welcomed. For form's sake, Kate wrapped the shawl around herself a little tighter. She waited for common sense to materialize along with the bracing breeze.

It didn't.

She took the few steps down to level ground. Maybe second thoughts could mount a defense.

"My car…" Her voice trailed off as she looked at the vehicle, parked to the rear of the lot.

"I can have one of my people come and get it for you."

She looked at him as his words sank in. "You have people?"

"On occasion," he allowed. He wasn't the type who enjoyed being waited on hand and foot. But there was no denying that Rosa was a far superior cook than he could ever be. Or that Elsa could clean rings around him. And for that, he paid them handsomely. "Or I can drive you back here later. Or tomorrow," he amended. Jackson watched her expression. "The choice is yours."

Well, at least he wasn't one to push his advantage. And the advantage was certainly his to push. She wasn't exactly feeling like a bastion of strength at the moment. But she didn't want to seem dependent on him for anything. That included transportation. "I guess I can have a cab bring me back here later."

"There's a host of possibilities," Jackson agreed.

Their eyes held for a very long moment. "Yes," she replied, "I suppose that there are."

Lacing his hand through hers, Jackson gently guided her over to where his vehicle was parked. It was closer than hers, a pristine silver sports model from the Mercedes line. A convertible, currently its top was up. Kate appreciated sleek lines.

"Nice car," she told him as they approached it.

Jackson unlocked the passenger door for her and held it open. "I've always had a weakness for beautiful things," he confessed with a smile.

Again, his eyes met hers.

The man was smooth, Kate thought. Very smooth. And these were just lines, nothing more. Handsome men had lines. But for the small space of time while they hovered in the air between them, she allowed herself to believe those lines.

"This is where you live?" Kate cried incredulously, her mouth all but falling open as they approached his current address. "It looks like something out of Mansions R Us." From where she stood, the building appeared to go on forever. "When do the tours go through? Or are they over for the day?"

The gates parted to admit them as Jackson punched out a code on his remote. "It's not that big," he protested with a laugh.

The driveway was bigger than the house where she'd grown up. "Not compared to a small country, no," she agreed, "but I think Rhode Island could certainly get lost in here."

Rather than house it in the two-storied, ten-car garage, he decided to park his vehicle in the driveway.

Getting out, he rounded the trunk and reached Kate's side just as she opened her door. "I guess it doesn't seem that big to me because I grew up here. This is my parents' house."

Swinging her legs out, Kate took the hand that he offered. There was such a thing as carrying independence too far and she had always liked chivalry.

Given that bit of information, that it was his parents' house, she looked at the building with a slightly different viewpoint. "Does that mean that your brother lives here?" she asked, curious.

He silently blessed his parents for their foresight. "My parents bought Jonah his own place about fourteen years ago." They walked up to the front door and he punched in another set of numbers on the keypad in order to disarm the security code for ninety seconds. "Mother didn't approve of his lifestyle and she knew there was nothing she could do to change him."

"Out of sight, out of mind?" Kate guessed.

Jackson's grim smile told her she was right. "You do what you have to do in order to make it through the day." With that, he opened the door for her and allowed Kate to walk in first.

It was like entering a completely different world. She dealt with wealthy clients all the time and she and her family were far from poor themselves, but this was a step above that. More accurately, several steps above that.

"So you live here alone?" she asked. The very foyer was larger than her first apartment had been. "Do you have to drop breadcrumbs to find your way back to the front door every morning?"

"Haven't had to do that for a while," Jackson responded with as straight a face as he could muster. Taking her hand, he nodded toward the rest of the house. "It doesn't bite," he promised.

Maybe, but the big question is, do you? she silently wondered.

Each step she took just made the house seem bigger to her. It was even larger on the inside than it had promised to be from the outside. "If you speak up, does your voice echo in here?"

"A little," he allowed. His eyes crinkled slightly in fond remembrance. "As a kid, I used to pretend this," he indicated the foyer, "was the gateway to another kingdom. Over there," he pointed to the left where the hall turned a corner, "was where the evil dragon lived. I used to have to slay him every afternoon if I wanted to make it up to my room."

She could visualize him fighting the fiery dragon. Knowing that he had the same kind of fantasies as any little boy made him seem more accessible to her. And just that much more appealing. "An eternally regenerating dragon. Must have been a big challenge for a small boy. How old were you?"

"Thirty. No, I'm kidding," he said quickly when she stared at him. "I was around eight." He grinned and the years seemed to fall away from him like layers of exfoliated skin. "I've never told anyone that before," he confessed.

"Afraid they'd think you were a little off?" she guessed, trying to maintain a light tone. In reality, she was very touched that he'd included her in this stroll through his young life—if, of course, he wasn't just making it all up as he went along. She tried to remind herself that the rich, as the old book title declared, were "different from you and me." Did that include the way they felt about people?

"Something like that," Jackson affirmed. He guided her to the entertainment center, the well lit one, not the one that looked like a mini movie theater. "My mother's imagination only ran toward suspecting my father of having affairs with different women. My father's imagination was taken up by coming up with excuses he could give my mother explaining why he was gone so much. They weren't all that good," he confided. "An eight-year-old kid could see right through them, let alone a highly intelligent woman who had graduated from Wellesley."

She caught her lower lip between her teeth, torn between feeling sorry for Jackson and wanting to just gloss over this because she instinctively knew he wouldn't welcome pity. "Doesn't exactly sound like people whose lives would have made glowing episodes for a family-channel drama."

He nodded. "More like something you'd find on one of the darker cable channels," he agreed.

Jackson knew that his jaded view of marriage and his desire to keep things light in any relationship had their roots in what he'd witnessed as a boy. That compounded with the way he'd felt when Rachel was killed were largely responsible for his no-strings-attached, seemingly carefree bachelor life.

Kate was still taking in her surroundings with no small awe. "And these 'people' you mentioned before, the housekeeper and the cook, are they here now?" Even if they were, she doubted she would be able to see them. This place had so many square feet to it, a person could easily meander around for days without encountering another soul.

Jackson shook his head. "No, they're off for the night. They don't live on the premises."

She looked around again, as if to reassure herself of the privacy. "Then we're alone in this huge place?"

"Completely." His grin was teasing as he drew a little closer to her. "Afraid?"

She wasn't about to lie to him. "Maybe just a little." Kate wasn't talking about the house, she was talking about the two of them. More accurately, about herself and the very strong attraction she felt for Jackson. Chemistry had always been her undoing.

Silent for a moment, he read between her lines. "I can take you back to Swift's parking lot," he offered kindly.

That was when he cinched his argument. Kate turned around to face him.

"Don't you dare," she warned, her purse sliding from her fingertips. The next second she wrapped her arms around his neck. And then, before she could rein herself in, her lips were on his, igniting the smoldering embers that existed between them.

The flash was inevitable. And immediate.

The second their lips met, Kate knew she wasn't going home tonight. Knew that she had been too long without engaging in physical contact with a man, too long without the feel of strong arms around her, sealing her to someone.

Sealing her away from viable thoughts.

All she had to do was remember that this wasn't serious. This was just for pleasure.

Her body began to vibrate inside, sending out shock-waves even as she felt the kiss deepening.

But if she felt that she could exercise any measure of control over the situation by being the one to initiate the first move, she had thought wrong. Because the second she kissed him, she found herself free-falling through time and space and spinning completely out of control, all at the same time.

It was as if someone had deliberately put a match to her face, to her skin and her body. The very essence of what made her who and what she was, was blazing hot—and only getting hotter.

It was crazy and she knew it. This was what she'd been

waiting for her whole life: a man who could effortlessly make her take leave of her senses and spin so far out of control that she was actually in another galaxy. Or at the very least, in a parallel universe.

She wanted to go fast, to grab everything she could and savor it before the moment was gone. Matt—the man she'd stupidly believed she was going to spend the rest of her life with—had made love as if the very house was burning down and he had to attain his pleasure and flee before it was too late. His goal was to climax, then relax, enjoying the sedativelike effect of an afterglow. Matt claimed it calmed him more than an after-dinner drink. Putting her on some kind of equal footing as popular wines, whisky and vodka.

So it was with great surprise that she heard Jackson softly whisper into her hair, "Slow down, Kate. What's your hurry? We have all night."

His very breath danced along her scalp. It only helped to fuel the fire she felt in her belly.

Chapter Eleven

His words ringing in her ears, Kate drew her head back and looked at Jackson. "All night?" she repeated uncertainly.

Was he presuming too much? Jackson backtracked a little. "Unless you have to be somewhere else," he qualified.

Here, Kate thought, the unsettling effect of his lightly skimming hands along her body almost negating her ability to form any lengthy coherent thoughts. *I have to be right here.*

"No," she literally breathed the word out. "I don't have to be anywhere else."

The smile bloomed on his lips at the same time that it slipped into his eyes.

"Good," he murmured.

It felt as if the second half of the word touched her throat a half a beat before his lips did. And there was lightning. Lighting that continued striking in the very same place, over and over again. Making her pulse race and her body prime itself for what she fervently prayed was to come.

Jackson went on taking his time, postponing his own final attainment of rapture to pleasure himself in Kate's reaction. Undressing her an inch at a time, he excited himself even as he watched the very same thing happening to her.

It was a tango and he led her through all the steps carefully, patiently and with barely harnessed control. Kate made him want to abandon it all and just take her to the highest pinnacle, especially when he found his breath growing shorter and shorter, his blood rushing in his veins.

But Jackson was determined to draw this out, for her if not for him. He had an underlying suspicion that whoever had come before him hadn't fully appreciated the woman that Kate was. Had, instead, just regarded her as an interchangeable partner. Someone to be on the receiving end of his largess.

For an unguarded second, he felt angry for her. But anger had no real part in this dance. It was all about pleasure.

The way she responded to his touch, to his slow, deliberate exploration of the curves of her body, to his lips tracing the varied tantalizing tastes of her skin, awakened something inside of him, despite his best efforts to keep it simple. He wanted to try harder to bring her teasingly to the very peaks, drawing back a little so that her own appreciation could be relished to the fullest capacity by them both.

Jackson reveled in her reaction, savoring more, anticipating the next steps beyond his normal scope of involvement. This one was special.

It was like her first time, only much, much better. Her experience wasn't all that plentiful, the men she'd known hardly numbering beyond a handful, but everything she'd ever experienced paled in comparison to what her body enjoyed right at this very moment.

Young, vital, active and energetic, Kate could still hardly catch her breath. The depth and breadth of the sensations that Jackson introduced her to, the ones that he brought out in her body that she, heretofore, had never known existed, were beyond description.

All she knew was that she'd never felt anything this wondrous before.

Don't get carried away.

She heard the little voice in her head, but she didn't obey.

Just as she didn't think that her body could sustain one more burst of raw ecstasy, she felt Jackson provocatively drawing his body up along hers until their interlocking parts were aligned.

Lacing his fingers with hers, pivoting on his elbows,

Jackson looked down into her face, a smile on his own. The very next moment, he was slipping into her, making them one.

The hypnotic expression in his eyes captured her soul. She couldn't have looked away if her life depended on it. And then he began to move. At first slowly, achingly, tantalizingly slow, and then she felt his hips moving against hers, the tempo growing faster and faster. Just the way his tongue had earlier when he'd anointed her and made her climax the first time.

What little breath she had left caught in her throat as Kate hurried to keep up, hurried to reflect the heat he gave off. If she was going to burn up, then so was he.

The need inside of her was almost overwhelming, taking her by storm.

Kate tightened her arms around him, sealing every part of her glistening body to his. The vague thought occurred to her that the heat generated would fuse them together permanently. If this was the end—and how could her heart ever go back to beating normally after this—it was all right with her. What a wonderful way to go.

When the final crest was conquered, Kate dispensed the last of her breath in a huge, satisfied sigh, weakly sinking back into the cushions of the oversize sofa. Her heart continued hammering.

The last of the swirling sensations faded and Jackson's grip around her body loosened ever so slightly. But he didn't withdraw his arms, didn't retreat. He didn't want to. He wanted to hold her to him. Wanted to feel the reassuring beat of her heart against his.

A sense of awe slipped over him. The world hadn't disintegrated despite the fact that these feelings that had been slamming through him were very new to him. Something had happened here. Logically, he needed time to assess. To regroup. And yet…

And yet the desire to do it again gathered strength, albeit not as swiftly as he would have wanted. That didn't change the fact that he *did* just want to hold her. Possibly for the rest of the night, or the rest of his life, whichever came first.

Kate raised her head slightly in order to look him squarely in the face.

He couldn't read her expression.

"Something wrong?" he asked. Had he hurt her? Was she upset? Lovemaking with a new partner was a little like walking across a tightrope. Exhilarating, but exceedingly tricky.

"No, I just wanted to see if you fell asleep." She'd come to expect that as a norm. And he still had his arms around her. If he hadn't fallen asleep, why were they still around her?

Jackson laughed quietly. He was far too wired, despite the exhaustion, to fall asleep any time in the near future.

"Not likely," he told her. And then her question echoed in his brain, generating questions of its own. "Why? Did the last guy you were with fall asleep?" He could see the answer in her eyes. This woman had awakened every fiber of his body. How could her last partner have fallen asleep on her? "Was he narcoleptic?"

"No. Just typical," she replied. "At least, I thought that was typical until just now."

Jackson threaded his fingers through her hair, gently pulling them through in order to caress her cheek. "Any complaints?"

For a second, she thought he meant about her past lovers and she was ready to give him a resounding "yes," but then she understood the focus of his question.

"About this? No. God, no," she said with feeling. She couldn't stop smiling. "On a scale of one to ten, you're fifteen."

He laughed, charmed by her and also, admittedly, a bit bemused. He wasn't sure whether just to enjoy his reaction to her or be worried by it. "I wasn't looking for a rating."

"I know," she answered. "That's what made it so good."

Jackson tried to piece things together. He drew himself up on his elbow, studying her expression. "That last guy, he asked you to rate him?" he asked in disbelief.

"Not in so many words, but…" Her voice drifted off, letting him make his own assumptions.

He drew her to him again. "Well, no offense, but whoever that last clown was, all I can say is that you're damn well better off without him."

Her eyes smiled as she reined in a desire to run her hands along his chest, his face, his body just for the feel of him.

Don't let yourself get carried away. You won't be disappointed if you don't get carried away.

"I know," she said aloud.

The sigh that escaped as she said the two words was pregnant with meaning. "You want to talk about it?" Jackson asked her. "I'm pretty good at listening."

"You probably are," she agreed. "Don't take this the wrong way, but this is just a little bit weird, talking about Matt while I'm lying here, naked, next to you."

Jackson didn't say anything. Instead, he tugged down the crocheted, cream-colored throw and gently covered her with it.

"There," he pronounced, tucking the edge around her. "You're as respectable as a pious grandmother on her way to daily mass." His smile was encouraging. "You can talk now if you want to."

Kate laughed and shook her head at the description. "Not quite that respectable."

"You can still talk," he urged, his voice low, coaxing.

"No point in talking," she answered. "I just wasted thirteen months on someone who turned out not to be worth ten minutes of my time. Why should I bother wasting any more?"

That meant the man in her past was either a cheat, or he had refused to commit. Possibly both since the two were by no means mutually exclusive. Jackson went with the first. "He cheated."

She noticed that Jackson didn't ask, he stated. Since he had, Kate saw no point in framing a denial. "Yes, he did. The worst part of it was it seemed like everyone else knew he was cheating—except for me." She pressed her lips together. Without realizing it, she moved even closer into Jackson as she relived the awakening moment. "Until I caught him."

Jackson winced in sympathy. "You threw him out, I hope."

"That would have been awkward," she confessed. "It was his house. I was the one who walked out. Ran, actually."

He kissed the top of her head. "The effect's the same."

Jackson probably didn't realize how sweet he was, she thought. He didn't have to be like this. She'd already gone to bed with him. Hell, it had been pretty much her idea.

"Yeah," she agreed. "Total devastation."

"I could see why he would be."

"No, I meant—" Kate raised her head to get a better look at his face. "Do you practice these lines, or do they just come to you when you need them?"

Jackson answered her question with an observation. "You're very suspicious."

"I'm sorry if I offended you, Jackson, but the fact is, if you get burned playing with matches, you start to view matches in a whole different light," she told him grimly.

"Matches can also be very useful," he pointed out, his voice low, sensuously seductive as he began to lightly and slowly strum his fingers along the slope of her body. "Once struck, they can give light to the shadows and chase away the dark. They can light a fire that in turn can cook your food, make your coffee, sterilize medical instruments…"

She held up her hands. "Cease. Desist," she requested. "I get it." And then she laughed. "How is it you wound up becoming a banker? With that tongue of yours, you could undoubtedly sell refrigerators to the Eskimos."

Jackson shook his head. "Too hard to lug around the inventory," he deadpanned.

She began to laugh, then stopped. Kate could feel her blood stirring again. Could feel the longing whispering along the perimeter of her senses, asking for an encore. Begging for it, really. Her eyes began to flutter shut. Not from fatigue but from the need to focus completely on the mushrooming source of her desire.

"I really wish you'd stop doing that," she told him with effort.

He was surprised by the intensity of his desire for her. Almost more than the first time.

"Not that I'm not prepared to do—or stop doing—anything you ask, but you do seem to be enjoying it. Exactly why do you want me to stop?" he asked.

Her breath was growing short again. This man had the most incredible effect on her, she thought. "Because I'm finding it difficult to keep my mind on what I'm saying."

His smile was positively wicked. "Why? Where's your mind going?"

She tried to draw in a long breath. It didn't work. And there went her pulse again, breaking records. "You know where my mind's going."

He ran his hand along her cheek, watching as her pupils grew as swiftly as sunflowers. "Tell me," he coaxed, his breath feathering along her skin, making a chill shimmy up and down her spine.

Any second now, she was going to jump on him if he didn't retreat. "You're making me want to make love with you again."

A mischievous grin curved the corners of his mouth. Just for a fleeting moment, she thought she saw something in his eyes. But it was gone before she could identify it.

"Done." Jackson slipped his hand underneath the throw.

The second he touched her, she was his for the taking—and glad of it. Signs of his wanting her were quite evident. Kate's eyes widened as she looked at him in surprise. "You can do that?"

Amusement wove its way through his response. "I'm not quite sure I know what you mean by 'that,'" he confessed.

Embarrassed, she made the best of it. "Make love more than once."

Jackson didn't answer her immediately. That was because he was processing the full extent of her words and her amazement. And then it all sank in.

"Oh, honey," he told her, wondering just what kind of Neanderthals she'd previously stumbled across, "you've been with the wrong men."

With one snap of his wrist, the crocheted throw was history, thrown back over the rear of the sofa. She wasn't going to be needing it, Jackson reasoned. He was the one who would be keeping her warm. He fully intended to show Kate just how much and how long he could continue to do "that" for a second time.

"Well, it's about time."

It was all Kate could do to swallow the scream that came barreling up her throat to her lips. Up until a second ago, she'd been trying to enter her office without calling any attention to herself and thus to the fact that she was coming in a full hour later than she was supposed to.

The greeting told her that she hadn't succeeded.

Swinging around, a fabricated excuse at the ready, Kate saw that the greeting had come from her brother who had made himself at home on the sofa in her office. For some reason, he was waiting for her. Why?

She realized that the palm of her hand was spread out protectively over her chest. Self-conscious, she dropped it.

"Look, I know I'm late, but that's no excuse for you to give me a heart attack," she accused. Forgoing her usual routine, she dropped her purse to the floor and sank down into her chair. She must have slept all of about twelve minutes last night and she was beat. She hadn't felt like this since college.

"Your late, less than dramatic entrance wasn't what I was referring to by saying it's about time," Kullen told her. "I'm assuming, since you look as if you literally ran into your clothes in order to get here before noon, that you finally hooked up with someone. *That's* what I thought was about time," he explained. The grin on his lips threatened to take over his entire face and then some. "Good for you, Katie."

She gritted her teeth at the nickname, but let that go for now. She believed in picking her battles and this one wasn't it.

"That's what you're basing your assumption on?" she asked incredulously, hoping that a display of enough bravado would make him back away. "That I look as if I dressed fast?"

"That," he allowed, "and the fact that I swung by your place last night and you weren't home. In case you're interested, it was after eleven."

"Eleven o'clock?" she echoed. "What if I was asleep?"

Kullen eyed her, his meaning crystal clear as he asked, "Were you?"

She should have remembered who she was dealing with. The Playboy of the Western World. Kate rolled her eyes. "This isn't the time or place to discuss our private lives."

"Evasion." Satisfied, Kullen nodded. "I have my answer."

She didn't like him reading her like a book. A woman was entitled to have secrets. "You do not," Kate insisted.

"Sure I do." He laughed. "If it was no, you would have said so. Instead, you evaded. Point made, case closed."

He wanted to play it this way, fine. "No," Kate declared, crossing her arms before her chest.

"Too late," Kullen crowed. "I fed you your line. Doesn't count." He was on the edge of his seat now, his hands clutching the armrests. There was glee in his eyes as he asked, "Do I know him?"

"You may not know anyone in a couple of minutes," she threatened. "Don't forget, I was the one Uncle Charlie told all his war stories to and taught how to sneak up on a man and silently render him dead."

Kullen did not seem the least bit intimidated. Rising, he made his way to the door.

"Spunky," he pronounced, nodding his head as he gave her one last look over. "Must have been one hell of a night. Good for you," he repeated just before closing the door behind him.

And just in time to avoid the box of tissues she threw at him. They hit the door and fell to the ground with a thud.

The moment her brother was gone, a wide grin spread out over Kate's lips. Bits and pieces of last night came back to her.

It had been one *hell* of a night, weaving its way into the early morning and taking her—and Jackson—with it.

George Bernard Shaw's fictitious Eliza Doolittle, once she found herself the subject of the famous musical, might have wanted to "dance all night" but as for her, Kate far more preferred the seductive dancing between the sheets that she and Jackson enjoyed into the wee hours of the morning and beyond.

Kate found that no matter how hard she tried to look serious, she just couldn't stop smiling. After a beat, she surrendered herself to the feeling.

Chapter Twelve

"Oh honey, where did you find him, is he taken and can I have him?"

The words emerged like rapid-fire gunshots from Jewel's mouth as she spoke to Kate on her cell phone. She made the call the moment her two-o'clock appointment with Jackson Wainwright was over and she was back in her car.

On her way back to the office from the courthouse where she'd been for the last two hours, taking a deposition, Kate pulled over to the side of the road outside a residential area the moment she heard her phone ring. She was certain it was Jewel and she wanted to hear what her friend had to say, not the least of which was her opinion of Jackson.

Kate addressed Jewel's questions in order. "He's one of Kullen's overflows. Not that I know of. And you'll have to ask Jackson that."

Although she had known Jewel all of her life and had shared almost everything with her and Nikki, Kate wasn't about to mention the fact that she had slept with the man. At least not for a while. Since both Nikki and Jewel were well aware of her last boyfriend debacle, she knew Jewel would attach undue importance to Jackson.

Suppressing a sigh, Kate did her best to sound businesslike. "Do you think you can help him?" she pressed, wanting to get Jewel to focus on something else other than Jackson's looks and availability.

Jewel had the kind of instincts that made her a natural for her chosen career.

"Shouldn't be a problem," she assured Kate. "He gave me the names of all the employees at the branch in question. In this handy-dandy age of the so-called privacy act, all the information is out there in cyberspace, waiting to be plucked. Finding out if one of those people is living beyond their means, or is suddenly writing big checks that need covering shouldn't be much of a challenge."

And then Kate could hear the smile creeping into Jewel's voice. "The bigger question is, can you get Kullen to send some 'overflow' in my direction? Kate?" Jewel queried when there was no response. "You still there?"

She didn't answer Jewel immediately because she

was weighing the pros and cons of her next move. "Yes, I'm still here." Oh, hell, Jewel would find out sooner or later—knowing Jewel, it would be sooner. "Look, you might as well know that my mother had a hand in sending Jackson to Kullen."

"Why would she have sent him to Kullen?" Jewel asked, confused.

"Actually," Kate clarified, "it was a mix-up. My mother, obviously a frustrated Mata Hari with no available outlet and no country to spy for, steered Jackson to my firm and told him to ask for K. Manetti."

Now it made sense. "And they connected him with Kullen."

"Exactly."

"So how did you get him?"

"You know my mother, she's never been very good at being patient—"

Jewel commiserated. "Gives her a lot in common with my mother."

"Anyway, from what I've pieced together, Mother must have called Kullen to ask if I'd gotten any new clients. When she found out that he was about to see Jackson, she undoubtedly ordered him to pass the man to me."

She heard Jewel laugh. "Gotta say that's better than getting a gift certificate to one of the stores in the mall."

For a private investigator, Jewel was certainly missing the obvious. "Jewel, she's meddling."

"She's a mother," Jewel pointed out. "It's what they

do. At least this one's a hunk—" And then she came to a skidding halt. "Wait a minute, then he is taken."

That was one hell of a conclusion Jewel had just jumped to. More importantly, she didn't want Jewel even to hint at that assumption the next time she spoke to Jackson.

"Not by me," Kate said with emphasis.

If she'd hoped that Jewel would drop the subject, she should have known better. "You said that a little too fast, Kate. *Is* something going on between you two?"

Kate evaded the question. "He's a client, Jewel. He needed a trust fund reinstituted."

The chuckle she heard on the other end of the line told her that Jewel wasn't about to be diverted. "Did you reinstitute anything else for him?"

"What does that even mean?" Kate wanted to know.

Jewel sighed. "If I have to explain that to you, Manetti, I guess the answer's no."

She did *not* want to continue in this vein. "Just get him the answers he needs."

"Did you ever consider that maybe the answer he needs is the word *yes?*" Jewel asked.

Dear God, Jewel was worse than her mother, Kate thought. "This conversation is getting too convoluted for me. I've got to go." Kate terminated the call before Jewel could say another thing.

Kate sat on the side of the road for a moment longer, frowning as she stared off into space. She'd spent quite possibly the best night of her entire life with the most incredible lover she'd ever encountered. Even so, she was afraid to let her thoughts go any further. Love was the easiest word in the world to say. Meaning it, well, that was a completely different matter.

Kate knew she couldn't allow her thoughts to drift into unchaperoned corners. She was afraid of the disappointment that she'd encountered time and time again. She had no desire to go that route again.

If she just kept everything in perspective, it'd be all right. *She'd* be all right, Kate silently insisted.

Meanwhile, she had work to do and a set of papers to deliver to Jackson.

The thought of seeing Jackson made her work faster.

Jackson was quiet for a long time as he read through the papers that he had already familiarized himself with when she'd brought them to him in rough-draft form. Everything seemed pretty ironclad.

Jonah wasn't going to be happy. That was a given. But at least his brother would be taken care of and he wouldn't wind up penniless—which was where he'd be, sooner than later, if he were allowed to spend his money unchecked. This trust fund was a way to rein him in—and keep him solvent.

Jackson put the papers down and raised his eyes to look at Kate. She hadn't been out of his thoughts for a single moment since she'd left his place two days ago. Two days and the longing for her had grown more intense, not less. He was unnerved because it made him feel so alive.

Remember Rachel and what that did to you.

He was in big trouble, he concluded. So why did he feel like smiling all the time?

"Perfect," he told Kate.

"I'm glad you're happy with it. Everything is as we'd discussed."

He wasn't talking about the documents. He was talking about her. But that was something, he knew, that was better left unexplained. Instead, he turned his attention to something else that had been on his mind.

"I'm thinking of having a will drawn up."

"A will?" she asked. Was he being responsible, or was there something more to this? Had he seen a doctor lately who had given him unwanted news?

"I know it sounds gruesome," Jackson continued, "talking about a will, but if anything happens to me, I don't want my money tied up in some incredibly lengthy legal battle."

She should have realized, Kate told herself, relieved. Jackson was just being Jackson, thinking ahead. "Understandable—and for the record, it's not gruesome," she told him. "It's very clear-sighted of you. A lot of people put off having a will drawn up because they think that once they do, it's like sending out an open invitation to God to be smitten."

The corners of his mouth curved as he looked at her. "Oh, I think I'm already that."

Kate felt a blush heating her cheeks and creeping up her neck. She struggled to bank it down.

"I'm using the word in the biblical sense," she told him.

The smile turned into an almost boyish grin. "Wasn't that what we were doing the other night, getting to know each other in the biblical sense?"

She didn't stand a fighting chance against the blush. Veins of heat shot up all through her body now. And all because he'd stood up and walked around behind her, brushing up against her.

"You're making it very hard for me to concentrate and keep my mind on business, Jackson."

Hearing that pleased him. "Good, then you're not tired of me yet."

He *had* to be kidding, she thought. The man had a mouth like sin and a positively wicked technique. If they lived to be a thousand, she knew *she* wouldn't be the one to ever grow tired of him. It would be the reverse, something she didn't want to think about even though it was inevitable. And sooner rather than later. She'd been through it enough to have that point driven home. Drop-dead gorgeous men liked to make the rounds.

Kate took a deep breath to steady her shredding nerves. She was a professional, a lawyer. Time to act like one.

"I take it you'll want the will to emulate the terms of the trust fund." And then she elaborated what she meant. "Your brother doesn't get the principle, just a monthly allowance."

Jackson nodded. That was it exactly. "You read my mind."

She laughed softly. "Not exactly a superhuman feat in this case."

"What about now?" he asked, threading his arms around her waist and gently pressing a kiss to the side of her neck.

A squadron of goose bumps suddenly let loose all along her body. "Now you're making me want to do something that'll get me in trouble," she breathed. "We're working," she reminded him. She was being paid an hourly rate to be his lawyer, not his lover, although right at this moment, she would have gladly opted for the latter over the former.

"I don't call this work."

The feel of his warm breath along her neck made her crazy. God, but he made her want to rip off her clothes—and his.

Kate let out a shaky breath, fighting to keep from melting, from having her eyes drift closed. "Jackson…"

"I want to see you tonight," he told her, turning her around to face him. "Someone gave me tickets to that new musical that's previewing here before going to Broadway. How do you feel about people bursting into song in the middle of a conversation?"

Funny he should mention that, she thought. It was something that she felt like doing herself right now. "I happen to like musicals," she told him in as calm a voice as she could muster.

He seemed pleased. "Good, then it's a date. I'll pick you up at five-thirty."

That seemed rather early. Most plays began at around seven-thirty or eight. "Five-thirty?"

He nodded. "It's at the Ahmanson Theater in L.A. The play starts at seven-thirty, but if I remember correctly, L.A. traffic is like an all-out miniature preview of what hell is like."

She nodded. If anything, that was an understatement. "It's gotten worse."

"I can't make it any earlier than five-thirty," he told her, glancing at the schedule on his desk calendar. "I've got a meeting at three that can't be postponed. It's going to be touch and go as it is."

Although she liked the idea of seeing a play with him, in the final analysis, it really didn't matter. Kate would have been equally happy stuck in traffic with him.

But even to hint at something like that, she was certain, would make the man not just back away but run for the hills as fast as he could possibly manage. She would enjoy this while it lasted.

Kate glanced at her watch. She'd already lingered longer than she should have. "I have to get going."

"So do I." He paused for a moment, looking at her. "Would it be out of order if a client kissed his lawyer goodbye?"

The correct answer was yes. She knew that. Basic client-lawyer relations 101. But "yes" wasn't the answer she gave him. "It wouldn't be out of order, just not customary."

"A rebel, beautiful *and* intelligent. Terrific combination," he told her just before he kissed her.

She could have easily sunk into the kiss. Easily lost

herself as well as all track of time. But that, she knew, would lead to other things and they were, after all, in his office. Any minute, someone could knock and want to come in. How fast could he get dressed? she couldn't help wondering before she dismissed the whole thought as grossly unprofessional.

"I'll see you tonight," she murmured as she broke away.

Walking out, she began to count the minutes until five-thirty.

"Jonah, I can't just give you that kind of money." Jackson hated arguing with his brother. He and Kate were on their way out to dinner and he'd just stopped at his house to drop off the report that her friend had compiled for him.

Jonah had rung the doorbell just as they were about to leave again. Kate had exchanged a few words with his brother, who responded in single syllable answers, and then excused herself to give them privacy.

The moment she was out of the room, Jonah had pounced, asking him for close to fifty thousand dollars. Now.

Jonah glared now, his resentment swiftly becoming a viable entity. "You wouldn't have to if you and your lawyer girlfriend hadn't blindsided me and somehow stuck my money back into the trust fund. It's *my* money," he insisted.

They had already been through this two weeks ago, when Jackson had told his brother that he wouldn't be coming into the money he'd anticipated on his birthday.

Jonah had gone pale, then alternated between shouting and pleading, all to no avail. Running out steam, feeling wounded, he'd finally stormed out.

This visit had started out a little more civil, but it wasn't about to stay that way.

"I did it for your own good," Jackson insisted wearily.

Jonah glared at him. "Is that what you're going to say at the funeral? That you did it for my own good?" he shouted. "Don't you get it?" he demanded, vacillating between anger and fear. "I owe these guys big-time. And trust me, these are not the kind of guys you go around stiffing."

"Then why did you go into debt to them?" Jackson wanted to know.

"I wasn't planning on owing them money," Jonah cried. "I was planning on winning." Desperate, he tried to approach the problem from another angle. "Look, you're one of the guys in charge of that big bank you work for, aren't you?"

Jackson eyed his brother with mounting disbelief. "I can't just take the money to cover your debts."

"Not 'take,'" Jonah coaxed, *"borrow."* He flashed the same brilliant smile that had so often won over their mother.

It was wasted on Jackson. "Oh, and how are you planning on paying it back?"

The smile faded a little, giving in to the desperation in his eyes. "I'm good for it."

God but he felt tired, Jackson thought. All he wanted

to do was go out and eat with Kate, steal a little time alone, not fight the same losing battle over and over again with his brother.

"Jonah, you're not even good for coffee. Just how do you think you can pay back the kind of money you're asking me for?"

"I'm working on it," Jonah snapped defensively.

"Now there's a novel concept—work," Jackson noted sarcastically. "You could try working at a job for a change."

"Look, man, it's not my fault I'm blocked. The inspiration just won't come. I'm trying to loosen up," he insisted. "That's why I'm gambling. Gambling relaxes me."

"Oh, really?" Jackson shot back. "Well, you certainly don't look very relaxed to me."

"That's because you're giving me grief," Jonah retorted. "You stole my money, now you don't have the decency to float me a loan."

"There's no such thing as a loan to you, Jonah. This is me you're talking to. Jackson. The brother who's 'loaned' you a hell of a lot of money over the years. It's like pitching money into a black hole. Well, it's over. I'm not going to do it anymore," Jackson declared with finality. It wasn't a threat, it was a statement.

When all else failed, Jonah resorted to his old stand-by. Guilt. "Well, if these guys catch up with me, I guess all of your troubles'll be solved, won't they?" he prophesized.

Kate couldn't take it anymore. She'd been in the other room, politely waiting for the two brothers to hash things out. But their voices, especially Jonah's, carried and she could hear everything. The more she listened to the exchange, the more difficult it was for her to remain silent. This was escalating quickly. She had to say something before she exploded.

When she finally walked back into the living room, the conversation was so heated, neither brother even noticed her. Clearing her throat, Kate raised her voice. "Excuse me."

The expression on Jackson's face appeared strained as he turned in her direction. He was very nearly at the end of his rope. "Not now, Kate."

There was no way she was going to be swept away. "Yes, now."

A cynical smile twisted Jonah's mouth. "Is this where I get the benefit of your wisdom, too?"

Kate moved forward, putting herself between the two brothers as she faced Jonah. "Well, you certainly need to get someone's because apparently you don't have any of your own right now. If Jackson covers this latest debt of yours, what are you going to do?"

"Drop to my knees and worship you?" It ended in a question, as if he wanted to see if he'd guessed the response she was after.

"Wrong," she said flatly. "You're going to take the money to pay off the debt—"

Jonah looked at her as if she was mentally feeble. "Well, yeah, sure—"

Kate held up her hand to stop him from saying

anything more. "Let me finish. You're going to pay off the debt, *then* you're going into rehab."

His immediate reaction was anger. "I don't have a drug problem anymore."

"No, you have a gambling problem now," Jackson said, joining forces with Kate. "You just substitute one addiction for another."

"You are going to get yourself under control," Kate continued as if there'd been no interruption from either of them. "And you're going to paint again."

"You think I haven't tried to paint?" Jonah said, obviously offended.

"Yes, I think you haven't tried to paint," Kate replied calmly. "But you're going to. Okay, to review and continue, Jackson pays off your debt, you go into rehab, get yourself straightened out, join Gamblers Anonymous when you get out and every single day, you are going to work at getting your gift back. No excuses," she underscored.

Jackson looked at Kate with renewed appreciation and not a little admiration.

"And if I refuse to go to rehab?" Jonah challenged belligerently.

This time, it was Jackson who fielded the challenge. "I won't give you the money."

Jonah turned on him. "You'd let me get killed?" he asked hotly.

"I hope it won't come to that," Jackson said in a calmer voice than he'd used earlier. It belied the inner turmoil he actually felt. "I'm hoping that somewhere in there is still a piece of the brother I used to idolize."

Stumped, his back to the wall, Jonah shoved his hands into his pockets. His eyes shifted from Jackson to Kate and back again. "There's no other way?"

Kate shook her head. "No other way." Her voice was firm.

Jonah let out a shaky breath. "I guess I have no choice, then." He raised his eyes and glanced at Kate. "I've done this before, you know. Gone to rehab. This is the end result," he told her bitterly, indicating himself.

"This time it'll stick," Kate said with conviction.

Jonah laughed shortly. "You're some kind of cock-eyed optimist, aren't you?"

"Part-time," she allowed.

Jackson looked at his brother. "I liked the other women you dated better. They were bimbos who didn't interfere."

"I'm the family lawyer," Kate reminded him. "It's my job to see that things run smoothly for you."

Jonah sighed. "I could bully Mortie," he said with a degree of nostalgia.

A hint of a smile played along her lips. "I'm not Mortie."

"Yeah, I know." Shoulders slumped, Jonah gave in. "Okay, we'll give your way a try."

Kate smiled. "Glad to hear it."

Jackson said nothing, but she felt his approval as he slipped his arm around her waist. She assumed that wasn't something that he'd ever done with Mortie.

Chapter Thirteen

Jackson leaned against the door he had just closed and watched Kate for a long moment.

"Do you have any idea how incredibly sexy you look to me right now?" he asked. Jonah had just left, a check in his pocket. That had been Kate's doing, as had Jonah's promise to enter rehab. If his brother reneged, the check would immediately be rendered null and void.

The woman was definitely a ray of sunshine in his life—in both their lives, Jackson silently amended. He was beginning to forget what life was like without her.

"No, actually, I don't." And then Kate smiled that inviting smile of hers. "But I'm hoping that you'll tell me."

He crossed to her, a wicked smile on his lips. "Better yet, I can show you."

"Better yet, you can show me," she agreed, her smile entering her eyes.

Jackson laced his fingers through hers and then began to gently guide her toward the stairs. "You know, I never would have thought that a bossy woman could turn me on." He glanced over his shoulder and winked at her. "I was wrong."

Kate glanced over *her* shoulder toward the front door. "Aren't we going in the wrong direction?" she asked more seriously.

He stopped for a moment. "You want to make love in the driveway?" he teased.

"No," Kate laughed, "but didn't you say you had reservations for dinner at The Belle of the Mississippi?" The exceedingly popular restaurant was usually heavily booked.

"I did. I do, but I can get new ones," he assured her. He was coaxing her up the stairs, taking one step at a time because he was going up backward in order to face her. "I know people."

"And if these 'people' you know say, 'Sorry, Jack, we're all booked up'?" she teased.

"First of all, nobody calls me Jack. And second—" Jackson lifted his shoulders in a careless, *que sera sera* gesture. "Worse comes to worst, there are leftovers in the refrigerator. Rosa made a pot roast yesterday," he told her.

"I *love* pot roast." Kate said it with such feeling he suspected that she wasn't really referring to the pot roast.

Jackson could understand her hesitation in making a real declaration about her feelings. He felt that way himself. He had feelings for her. He *knew* he had feelings for her. The hesitation occurred when it came to giving *voice* to those feelings. This was hard for him. He'd been in this place before and it had all blown up on him. He needed to go slow. Make certain that it was what it was and not something that would pass. Until he was sure, the less said, the better.

Or, what if he said it to her, told her he cared about her, and she only echoed the words back out of pity, or because it was too awkward not to?

Or, worse yet, what if she *didn't* echo the words? What if there was only silence hanging between them like some huge, unmanageable, blazing albatross?

"Yeah, me, too," he told her. "I love roast beef, too."

And for now, that would have to do. Until, at the very least, he had some kind of indication from her that it was all right to give voice to his feelings because she felt the same way.

The moment he drew Kate up to the landing, Jackson began undressing her. She'd thought that he would wait until they got into his bedroom. It thrilled her that she was wrong.

Laughing as he slid the zipper down her back, she twisted out of range. "What are you doing?"

"Utilizing my time efficiently," he told her with a straight face.

The next moment, he swept her up into his arms and pressed his lips to hers, ending any further discussion, relevant or otherwise.

"You're sure?"

Sitting at his desk several weeks later, Jackson looked at the report Jewel had just brought to him. Kate was in the office, as well, but for the moment, he was only aware of the ambivalent feelings racing through him.

How was this possible? The person behind the missing funds was the last person he would have suspected.

That was why it was possible. Because the thief looks so innocent.

"I'm sure," Jewel assured him.

Technically, her work had been concluded when she finished compiling the financial scan of the branch tellers' accounts and their current spending histories. But, being Jewel, she had gotten engrossed in the problem and gone the extra mile.

More accurately, the extra *several* miles. She'd continued conducting the investigation to satisfy her own curiosity because she'd come across suspicious dealings that had piqued her interest. And she had been right.

Jackson glanced up at her after reading the second page. "It says here that Elena Ortiz was turned down by

Lincoln Mutual for her request for a loan of fifteen thousand dollars."

Jewel nodded and summarized the rest of her report. "Elena goes to this fast-food restaurant on the corner of Alton and Jeffrey every Friday at one o'clock. She gets a soda and sits down at one of the tables. In a few minutes, this man with the blackest hair I've ever seen joins her. They exchange a few words, then they exchange an envelope. She passes it to him," Jewel added before he could ask. "And then she gets up and leaves. She never finishes her soda."

Jackson gave voice to the first thing that came to his mind. "Blackmail?"

Jewel nodded. She glanced in Kate's direction before saying, "That would be my guess. I tailed him and copied down his license. The car's a rental. According to the rental agent, he always rents a different car on Fridays and he always pays cash."

"Didn't he have to show them his driver's license before he got the car?" Kate asked.

"He did and they had a copy on file. I flirted my way into getting a copy of my own." She looked at Jackson as she reached into her purse. "Want to see it?"

Jackson was already putting his hand out. "Absolutely." Jewel pulled the sheet out of her purse and gave it to him. Jackson read the name out loud. "Diego de la Vega."

Kate recognized the name instantly and frowned. "Looks like we're hunting Zorro." When Jackson looked at her, puzzled, she elaborated, "That was Zorro's Clark

Kent name. His secret identity," she explained, then sighed, frustrated. "Looks like this guy has a sense of humor."

"Maybe," Jackson allowed, his face grim. How far did this extend? Or was it just a two-character drama? "But I don't. Not when it has to do with stealing from the bank." He looked up at Jewel as he opened the middle drawer of his desk. "You've done a great job, Jewel. I really appreciate it." Taking out his personal checkbook, Jackson wrote down the fee they'd agreed on plus a bonus for her extra time and work. Finished, he tore the check out of his book and held it out to her. "Why don't you give me a few of your cards? I'll hand them out to people who might find themselves in need of a good private investigator with initiative."

"I'd appreciate that," Jewel told him, taking several cards out of her purse. They did an exchange, he taking the cards and she the check. When she glanced at the sum, she stopped. "You wrote it for too much."

"No," he contradicted, "I wrote it for the right amount." He smiled broadly at her. Because of her, he had his thief. The bank was safe again. "Thank you."

"Thank *you*," Jewel emphasized. Crossing to the door, she stopped for a second and looked at Kate. "I'll call you," she promised. The next moment, she was gone.

Kate nodded in response, but her mind wasn't on Jewel. It was on Jackson's teller and what was about to happen next. Her empathy instantly went out to the petite woman she'd met at the catered party Jackson had thrown. It felt like a million years ago now.

"Talk to her, Jackson," she urged.

His expression darkened ever so slightly. "Oh, I fully intend to."

She caught his tone instantly. "No, *talk* to her," she emphasized. "Find out what's going on. Give her a chance to explain," she implored.

He shifted to face her and she saw the contained anger. She knew him. Jackson felt responsible. He was in charge and anything that went wrong was on him. "I'll tell you what's going on. She's stealing."

"But there's probably a reason."

He shook his head, shutting her out. "Not my problem."

He began to walk toward the door and she put herself in his path.

"Technically," Kate underscored. "But this isn't just a bank teller," she insisted. "This is a *person*. Someone who doesn't look as if she'd steal unless it was a last resort."

His expression was impassive. "And you can tell all this by looking at her?"

She heard the unavoidable touch of sarcasm in his voice, but told herself not to take it personally. He was just upset.

"I have good instincts, at least in some areas," she amended, thinking of her penchant to be attracted to the wrong men until now—she hoped. "Call Elena in," she urged. "Talk to her." And then she thought of a better idea. "Or let me talk to her."

"Can't do that," he told her flatly. "You're my lawyer, not the bank's."

He had a point, but she wasn't giving up. "Then let me at least sit in."

What possible justification did she have for that? "As what, my conscience?"

Kate inclined her head. "If you wish." But she did have a better negotiating chip to play. "Think of it this way—if she decides to shout 'harassment,' I can be your witness to the contrary."

That at least was a valid argument, although he had a feeling that wasn't why Kate wanted to be there. She could temper him if need be. Did she believe he was going to roast the girl on a spit? "You won't give up, will you? Are you always this tenacious?"

"It's my job," she told him with a small smile. "Speaking of which, how's Jonah coming along?"

For the first time in a long time, Jackson felt he had reason to entertain a little hope. "He's scheduled to come out of rehab this weekend. I'm picking him up and having him stay with me for a while." He wanted to be there in case Jonah began to backslide. The moment he framed the thought, Jackson realized that he had used the words "in case," not "when." It felt good. "I'm trying not to be too optimistic, but he sounds really good," he confided.

"Be optimistic," Kate encouraged. "Show Jonah that you're rooting for him to succeed."

"Isn't that putting too much pressure on him? Jonah doesn't do well under pressure."

Kate naturally gravitated to the positive side. "Better that than his feeling that you're just waiting for him to mess up."

Jackson thought it over for a moment. "Maybe you're right," he allowed.

"Of course I'm right," Kate assured him cheerfully. "I'm your lawyer." She glanced toward the door and envisioned the tellers on the other side. "Now call Elena in."

Jackson put his hand on the doorknob, his mouth set grimly. Kate was glad he was letting her stay. She had a feeling she might be needed for moral support if nothing else.

Elena Ortiz was barely five feet tall and looked as if the only way she could come close to weighing a hundred pounds was if she had a friend stand on the scale with her. Her shoulder-length blue-black hair was as straight as a razor and she wore it up, as if to appear older than her twenty-two years.

Her brown eyes were huge as she walked into Jackson's office. She seemed fragile, as if she was ready to break in two at any moment.

"You wanted to see me, Mr. Wainwright?" she asked in a small voice.

"Yes, I did, Elena." Jackson gesture to the chair in front of his desk. "Please, sit down." He turned toward Kate and made the introduction. "This is my lawyer, Kate Manetti."

"Your lawyer?" Elena echoed nervously. She extended her hand to Kate only after the latter had put hers out first.

"I asked to sit in," Kate explained, instinctively knowing that the young woman would immediately think the worst and become frightened. Kate couldn't help feeling sorry for her. As if to confirm her suspicions, Elena's hand was icy cold when she shook it.

Jackson began his interview quietly. "Elena, are you happy here?"

Kate noted that a smattering of relief filtered into the young woman's eyes. Poor thing obviously thought this was an evaluation. Or at least she was praying for that.

"Oh yes, very happy," Elena responded with enthusiasm.

Jackson nodded and immediately got down to the heart of the matter. "Then if you are so happy here, why are you stealing from the bank?"

Elena's eyes widened and her face paled visibly. She looked as if she would pass out at any second.

"What? No, no, I'm not stealing," she cried. Distress vibrated in every syllable.

"There's no point in denying it, Elena," he said calmly. "I've had you followed." Her distress mounted prodigiously, every thought reflected in her face. "Who is the man you give envelopes to every Friday?"

Instead of answering, Elena covered her face with her hands and began to cry.

Kate couldn't maintain her silence. "If you tell us, we can help you," she interjected. She exchanged a glance with Jackson. He didn't seem all that pleased with her light touch. But she sincerely felt that coaxing instead of threatening would work best with the frightened young teller. "Elena, you have to talk to us."

After a beat, Elena raised her head. Tears streamed down her face. "If I don't give him the money, he will kill her."

"Kill who?" Jackson instantly demanded.

"My sister. Lupe." Every word seemed an effort for her. Sobs wove themselves through every breath she took. "I told her to wait. *Begged* her to wait. I said that I would send for her when I had the money." Her eyes shifted to Kate, appealing to her maternal instincts. "But she is seventeen and impatient." Elena pressed her lips together before going on. "She paid this organization to bring her into California."

"A coyote?" Kate guessed. Coyotes were cold-blooded men who charged a great deal of money to guide desperate people across the border in the dead of night. A good many never completed the journey. The desert was strewn with the bodies of former coyote clients.

But Elena shook her head. "No, he is part of some organization," she insisted. "They smuggle things." Then, to illustrate what she meant, she said, "Drugs, people. Prostitutes," she added in a lower, more horrified voice. It was obvious that this last term held special meaning for her. "That is my sister's choice. If I cannot pay them, she can let them kill her or become a prostitute. Either way, she is dead," Elena told them grimly.

"How much did they ask for?" Jackson asked. He had a tally of how much had gone missing over the last two months, ever since he'd taken over. He wanted to see if it matched what Elena was going to say.

"Fifteen thousand dollars. Fifteen thousand more," she corrected. "Lupe already gave them five thousand. I don't know where she got that money from," Elena confessed, despair vibrating in her voice. She was a woman on the verge of a breakdown, not knowing where to turn, what to do and needing to remain strong. It was obviously tearing her apart.

She raised her eyes to Jackson, pleaded. "I did not want to do this, Mr. Wainwright. I did not want to steal from the bank. I have always been a good person. But I have no money. I tried to borrow it, but I could not get a loan and she is my only sister—" Her voice broke as more sobs burst from her throat.

Unable to keep her distance any longer, Kate rose and came over to the young girl. She put her arms around Elena and held her.

"We'll get your sister back safe," she promised, stroking Elena's head. "And don't worry about the money. It will be put back."

"I will go to jail?" she asked fearfully, clearly hoping against hope that the answer would be no.

Kate didn't intend to add to the young woman's anguish right now. Elena was going through enough as it was. Kate could easily see how fragile her state of mind was.

"Something can be worked out." The moment she made the promise, she could feel Jackson looking at her. She'd succeeded in making him angry. That wasn't her intention, but she had a conscience to follow. A conscience that wanted to alleviate suffering, not inflict it.

"Right now," Kate continued, "we need to find a way to get your sister back and put this Diego de la Vega and his little organization out of business."

"I would be so grateful," Elena cried.

"Elena, would you mind returning to your station?" Jackson politely requested. "I need to have a few words with my lawyer."

Elena was instantly on her feet. "Yes, of course, Mr. Wainwright. And thank you, thank you both!" she cried with feeling.

The moment the door was closed, Jackson turned to Kate. She held up her hand before he could say anything. "I know what you're going to say."

"No," he contradicted, "I don't think you do." He wasn't angry about her usurping his position, or even that she'd made assumptions about what he was going to do. Right now, it was Kate's safety that troubled him. She was the type to sail into the eye of the storm, not away from it. "This isn't some episode from *Law & Order,* Kate," he told her. "These men think nothing of killing people. You can't deal with them. You can't try to reason with them. It's too dangerous."

Kate let out a huge sigh. "And I just got my cape out of the cleaners, too," she lamented mournfully. And then her expression instantly lightened. "Of course I know that these are dangerous men. All the more reason to get them off the street and into custody. I doubt that

Elena's sister is the first person they've held hostage for the purposes of extortion. And she's probably not the only one right now, either. But don't worry, I'm not about to go riding into their camp on a white horse.

"I do, however, know a few of the people working at the Immigration and Customs Enforcement department. After Elena pays this vermin the rest of the fifteen thousand and gets her sister back intact, the ICE agents will come charging in and arrest these bastards. Everything will be aboveboard and nice and legal." His expression told her he was far from convinced. Was he worried about her, or worried about the bank's reputation? That thought bothered her, but she couldn't tell. "Are you angry because I told her she wasn't going to jail?"

"That's not our decision to make," he told her.

"Sure it is. Because it's up to you to decide whether or not to call the police in about the embezzlement. You could say that it was just a record keeping error. A glitch in the software. That happens more times than you could believe."

"In other words, lie and cover up the theft." He set his mouth firmly.

"In other words, give someone a second chance," Kate corrected. "Elena was caught between the proverbial rock and hard place, Jackson. What if it was your sister those slime bags had? What if it was you who didn't have any money to save her?"

"I would have found another way."

She shrugged. "You're smarter."

"Now you're trying to flatter me into sweeping this under the rug?"

She smiled up at him brightly, the soul of innocence. "Is it working?"

"Call your friends at ICE. They're going to be in position to take this guy down the next time Elena has an envelope for him."

Mentally crossing her fingers, Kate took out her cell phone to make the call. But not before she kissed Jackson. Long and hard.

"What was that for?" he asked, recovering.

"Call it a retainer—for later," she told him with a wink as she began to tap out the phone number she needed on her cell phone.

Chapter Fourteen

The moment Jackson gave her the go-ahead sign, Kate did just that.

She lost no time in getting in contact with Agent Howard Brady. She'd gone to school with Howard, who had majored in languages, and had been friends with his wife, Shelly, before the two had ever gotten married. After college, they'd kept in touch via newsy Christmas cards, which was how she'd initially discovered that Howard now held down a fairly responsible position at ICE.

Meeting with Howard for lunch, Kate carefully sounded him out. She constructed a so-called hypothetical scenario in order to ask him what the department's stand was on Elena's situation. She knew, less than halfway through her narrative, that Howard was aware that the situation wasn't really hypothetical, but he played along anyway and heard her out.

With some cajoling, she finally managed to obtain a pledge of leniency from him. She had him put it in writing. They used the back of a napkin. When the "pledge" was safely in her purse, Kate gave him the rest of the details. She told Howard that as far as she could ascertain, the man holding Elena's sister hostage was either the head of an illegal human smuggling ring, or at the very least, one of the ring's main components.

"I can get him on a platter for you," she promised enthusiastically. "But only after he gives up where her sister's being held. If you grab him up before that, the girl is certain to be killed by one of his henchmen."

Howard was silent for a moment as he ate. "And this banking district manager, Wainwright," he finally said, "he can back up your story?"

"Every last syllable."

Finished, Howard pushed away his plate. "Okay, you have a deal."

Elena looked fearful when she was introduced to Howard, and even more so when Howard informed her that she would have to be wired for her next meeting with her sister's kidnapper. But with no other recourse open to her, she finally agreed. There was no other way to rescue Lupe.

Kate wanted to go with Elena for the last meet, but she

knew that if they deviated from the set formula, the man would turn and run and then Lupe would be lost to them.

"I will be fine," Elena told her, her voice quaking. Squaring her slim shoulders, she went into the fast-food restaurant alone.

A few minutes later, unable to just sit and wait, Kate entered, as well. She mingled with the customers who, at that time of day, were a cross section of blue- and white-collar workers, all intent on grabbing a quick, inexpensive bite for lunch.

The plan was that since this was the last payment, Elena told the former coyote that she had the envelope hidden in a safe place. She would give him the location once she was taken to where her sister was being kept hostage.

Grumbling, the trafficker cursed her several times over, then finally agreed to her terms. He told her that he would bring her to her sister.

And then his eyes drew together malevolently as he added, "But if you are lying about the money, it will be the last lie you ever tell—and the last breath your sister will ever take." With that, he grabbed Elena by the arm, yanked her out of her seat and roughly guided her out of the establishment.

Kate's heart had almost stopped when she glimpsed the look on the man's face as he passed her. Counting to five, she followed them outside, pretending to walk to her car.

Instead, she hurried over to a van with the logo of a local utility company slapped on its side. Howard and his partner were maintaining surveillance from inside the vehicle.

Glancing over to make sure that she wasn't being observed, Kate knocked once and got in. Howard's partner was already starting up the van.

"Let's go," Kate cried.

Howard looked at her, stunned. "You're a civilian. We can't take you with us," he protested.

"Think again," she'd retorted. "I'm responsible for that girl being in this position. You can't let her out of your sight and I'm not getting out. Now go!" Kate ordered.

Muttering words in a language she didn't understand, Howard tapped his partner on the shoulder. They were on the road a moment later.

In the end, it all turned out better than they could have hoped for, Kate thought, relieved beyond words. For a while there, the outcome had been touch and go. Once or twice, she'd come very close to jumping out of her skin. But when the smoke cleared, figuratively and otherwise, Howard and his partner had an impressive bust on their hands. Almost thirty girls had been rescued from a very grim fate. Best of all, Elena was reunited with her sister. It was a tearful reunion.

Because Kate as well as Howard had pulled a certain amount of strings, Lupe was going to be allowed to remain in the country in exchange for her testimony against the people who had smuggled her across the border. In addition, Elena would testify about the blackmail. There was no doubt that the traffickers were going away for a very long time.

Kate caught herself singing as she drove back to Jackson's office. Things couldn't have gone better, she thought happily. Jackson had wanted to come with them, but there was a scheduled meeting he couldn't postpone. She was now going to his office to fill him in.

At first, she didn't think anything was wrong. His meeting over, Jackson listened to her narrative attentively. He was a little quieter than she'd become accustomed to, but he did have a great deal to take in.

His expression darkened noticeably when she came to the part about getting into the ICE van and going with the agents as they followed Elena and the trafficker.

He hadn't heard her right. She couldn't be saying what he thought she was saying. The woman was smarter than that. "You did what?" Jackson demanded.

She was so wrapped up in her narrative that, for a moment, Kate didn't understand what it was that Jackson asked. Or why he sounded so angry. In the time they'd been together, she'd never seen that expression on his face before.

"I'm afraid I don't—" Kate didn't get a chance to finish.

"But you *did,* that's just it." Didn't she understand the kind of risk she'd taken? A completely *unnecessary* risk. The woman could have been killed.

A cold chill went down his spine, reminiscent of what he'd experienced when he'd learned about Rachel being run over in the crosswalk. Damn it, he couldn't go through this again, couldn't stand having his gut ripped out again.

"You're not supposed to go running down the street after human traffickers, especially the kind who would just as soon kill you as look at you."

Kate resented his tone. Resented, too, that he made her sound like some kind of empty-headed nitwit. "I didn't go 'running down the street' after him," she corrected tersely, "I was in a car."

One wrong move and she could have become just another memory. What the hell was wrong with her? And what the hell was wrong with him, opening himself up to unspeakable pain again?

"Like that's supposed to make a difference?" he snapped. "You shouldn't have done it. You should leave things like that up to the professionals."

Maybe the man still didn't know what made her tick, Kate thought. Maybe she didn't mean enough to Jackson for him to understand the kind of person she was.

Was he going to be another prince who turned out to be a frog? Had she been right all along, to be afraid that he'd be like all the rest? Oh God, her heart began to hurt.

Damn it, Mom, I told you this was going to happen. Why couldn't you just have left things alone? Why did you have to bring him into my life?

"I don't do standing on the sidelines too well," she ground out.

"Maybe you should learn." If anything had happened to her, he wouldn't have been able to live with himself. Wouldn't have been able to recover. If not for him, there was no way she would have gotten involved in this.

"Standing on the sidelines is your calling, not mine." The accusation came out before she could stop it.

Jackson's eyes narrowed. "What's that supposed to mean?"

She was *not* about to explain something he already knew. "I think it's self-explanatory." Her voice was cool in sharp contrast to the anger she was feeling.

He wasn't in the mood for games. It was all he could do to keep from shouting. "If it was, I wouldn't be asking, would I?"

Kate blew out an angry breath. Maybe he *was* that dense. "How long have we been seeing each other?"

Jackson felt as if he'd just been dropped in the middle of the forest in the dark—blindfolded. He knew the answer—almost seven weeks—but it had no bearing on her reckless act. "What the hell does that have anything to do with what we're talking about?"

Oh God, it was worse than she thought. He was completely oblivious, wasn't he? Or, more likely, he didn't care. How, after all she'd been through, could she have willingly walked into the same situation again? Even idiots learned from their mistakes.

"Everything," she retorted. "Where do you get off, telling me what I can and can't do?"

"I'm the guy you've been sleeping with." *The guy*

who loves you too much to survive having anything happen to you. He'd been right to try to protect himself. This wasn't going to work.

She was right. He *didn't* care. He just wanted to control her. No matter how much she wanted him to love her as she was, it wouldn't change anything. She was an idiot for ever putting her guard down. An idiot for loving him. It was final. Another prince had turned out to be a frog.

"Is that all that you are?" she challenged.

This whole conversation was getting convoluted and ridiculous. If he had to explain things to her, maybe there was nothing to explain, at least, not as far as she was concerned.

Exasperated, he cried, "What do you want from me?"

"Apparently more than you can give." She grabbed her purse and pushed the strap on her shoulder. "I have to go." She didn't wait for him to say anything. Instead, she crossed straight to the door. "I told Elena and her sister I'd be right back. I just thought you'd want to hear what happened."

"Kate—"

But she didn't stop, didn't turn around. Reaching the door, Kate marched out without another word. It took all she had not to slam the door in her wake. That would have been childish. It would have felt good, but it would have been childish. And the pain she felt didn't belong to a child.

She forced herself not to run, but it didn't matter.

Jackson didn't come after her, didn't call out. Didn't make any attempt at all to bring her back.

The pain in her heart grew more intense as she went on walking.

Jackson stared at the door that Kate had just closed in her wake. He was angry and utterly at a loss as to what had just taken place here. Until she'd walked in, he'd spent the entire morning feeling as if his whole life was being precariously balanced on the edge of a razor-sharp saber. More than once he'd upbraided himself for letting Kate go along with the agents and Elena for the last exchange. So many things could have happened to her. The last half hour before Kate arrived in his office, his head had been filled with recriminations as he cursed himself for not stopping her. Or, since she was determined to go, for not going with her, meeting or no meeting. But he had been needed here and in a moment of weakness, he'd kept his protest to himself.

But there were so many variables that went into comprising the scenario, so many things that could have gone horribly wrong. Even now, it made him sick to his stomach just to contemplate them.

Because the thought of losing Kate was too awful to think about. It was Rachel all over again. He'd barely survived that. He couldn't, *wouldn't* go through that again.

Even so, he could feel himself wavering. Jackson was torn between going after her to tell her everything that was in his heart—and just pulling back and cutting his losses. Reclaiming himself before he was hopelessly and forever lost.

The decision was taken out of his hands the next moment as his phone rang. Picking up the receiver, he heard the bank's vice president on the other end. His presence was needed at the Aliso Viejo branch.

His private life was being temporarily preempted by his professional one.

"I'll be right there," he promised.

Maybe this was for the best. Maybe he'd just been saved.

Kate did her best to remain in perpetual motion. She kept busy by helping Elena and Lupe square things away, smoothing out every possible feather that had been ruffled. She called in every favor she could to insure that the sisters would not ultimately be deported. In the interim, she worked with each to insure that their testimony against the traffickers went smoothly.

Even though he hadn't tried to contact her since she'd walked out of his office, Jackson was a man of his word. Kate was confident that Elena would not be charged with embezzlement. Kate believed her when Elena tearfully swore she would be grateful for the rest of her life.

"Just don't get into any more trouble," Kate warned affectionately. "And if you need anything at all, be sure to come to me." She'd pressed one of her business cards into Elena's hand. Elena held it against her heart as she waved goodbye when Kate drove off.

With that settled, Kate tried to fill every waking moment with work. She volunteered to pick up the slack at the firm, coming in early, staying late and helping the other lawyers put together briefs.

But eventually, she had to go home.

Home to an emptiness that slashed at her as painfully as any knife making contact with her skin.

She put the TV on the minute she walked in the door and kept it on until she left for work the following morning in an attempt to slay the silence.

She couldn't sleep, couldn't really eat.

This was ten times worse than when she'd fallen for Matt, she thought. She didn't know she could hurt this much. There was no place she could go to hide from the pain.

Jackson's sudden reversal of behavior had come without warning. Up until then, there hadn't been so much as a hint of this other side of him. All along, he'd been perfect. His sense of responsibility to his brother, his way of operating at work, the displays of charity, all of it shouted of a man who was decent and kind and good. Granted she'd gradually grown more and more concerned when he hadn't said anything about his feelings for her, but she'd tried to be patient, because everything good was worth waiting for.

But she'd gone on waiting. If he did have any deep feelings for her, he kept them to himself.

It was Jackson's presumption that he could order her around without verbalizing the least sort of affection for her that finally set her off.

Damn it, she thought, staring at the ceiling in her bedroom, watching shadows ebb and flow, when was she going to learn? Hadn't she been the one to profess that she was tired of kissing princes only to discover that they were actually frogs? How many times did that have to happen before she finally got the message?

The message that not everyone was meant to wind up with someone for life? Her lot fell in with that number, not with the starry-eyed, happily-ever-after crowd. The sooner she accepted that, the better.

Kate buried her face in her pillow and cried.

She'd been like this for two weeks now, feeling tears gather in her eyes for the third time that night as she wandered about her house like a ghost, unable to find a place for herself. She'd rebuffed all her mother's attempts to get in contact with her, claiming she was incredibly busy. She was *not* about to talk to her mother about Jackson and that was all her mother was interested in discussing.

If she didn't get more than ten minutes' worth of sleep soon, Kate thought miserably, she was going to fall apart.

Maybe she needed a prescription for sleeping pills. She really didn't want to have to go that route, but if she kept up like this, she was going to wind up driving up the wrong freeway ramp or something equally as disastrous. The idea of hurting someone else by accident chilled her heart.

First thing tomorrow, she decided, she was going to call her doctor and—

Was that the doorbell?

Finding herself in the kitchen, Kate stopped and listened. That *was* the doorbell.

She glanced at the clock on her microwave. It was almost eleven. Who'd be calling her no—

Oh God, no. Not now. She shut her eyes, searching desperately for strength. It was her mother, she just knew it. Since she couldn't get her on the phone, her mother had come in person.

Go away, Mom.

The doorbell rang again, longer this time. And then again for a fourth time. Kate sighed. She knew her mother. The woman was quiet but as tenacious as a pit bull when she wanted to be. Her mother would be leaning on that doorbell all night until she opened the door.

"All right, all right, I'm coming," Kate shouted as she made her way to the living room. "Did it ever occur to you that I might be sleeping?" she demanded, looking through the peephole.

"Were you?"

The voice on the other side of the door was a great deal deeper than her mother's. And with good reason. It wasn't her mother.

It was Jackson.

"Your mother sent over chicken soup," he announced, holding a container aloft so that she could see it through the peephole.

That got her to open the door. "You went to see my mother?" Kate demanded incredulously. He didn't bother calling her, but he was socializing with her mother?

"Since you didn't come with an instruction manual, I needed to talk to someone wiser than me because I needed help." He offered her the container. "She thinks you can use this."

Taking the container, Kate put it aside on the hall table. "Help you what?" she asked, vacillating between wanting to throw her arms around him and wanting to strangle him. The internal tug of war caused her to remain where she was.

"Can I come in?" he asked.

Kate sighed, opening the door wider. "Sure," she said with no emotion. "Come in." She shut the door, struggling to ignore the fact that her heart had just launched into double time. "Help you what?" she repeated.

God, but he had missed her, Jackson thought. Missed the sight of her, the scent of her. He hadn't lied. At a loss, he'd sought out her mother to enlist her help as to how to get the woman he loved back. Because he'd made a huge mistake, thinking he could just shut down and walk away. It was too late for that. He loved her and he wanted her in his life. Five minutes, five years, five decades, it didn't matter, he'd take what he could get.

Right now, he wanted to touch her, to hold her, but this needed to be resolved first. "Help to find a way to apologize."

"Do you have any idea what you're apologizing for?" *He's here, don't put him through the Spanish Inquisition.* God, that was her mother's voice in her head. She'd officially gone over the edge.

The corners of his mouth curved just a little. "For pushing you away because I was afraid of how I'd feel, losing you."

"Maybe it's because I haven't had any sleep, but that doesn't make any sense," she told him.

"Yes, that's why I went to your mother. Because I can't do this."

She *really* wasn't following him. "Do what?"

"Face another day without you in it."

Oh God. She wasn't going to melt, she chastised. Not yet, not until she heard him tell her what she needed to hear. "That's a good start. Go on," she encouraged.

"I don't have a speech—"

"I wasn't asking for one," she told him softly, then gave him a small hint. "I was asking you to tell me what you were feeling."

That was easy enough. The hollowness was killing him. "Empty. Lost. Lonely."

"And?" she coaxed.

"And if you don't come back, I don't know what I'm liable to do."

"Because?"

Frustration momentarily got the better of him, but Theresa had counseled him to be honest. To let his heart do the talking. So he did. "When you told me that you'd gone with those agents, all I could think of was that I could have lost you just like that, in the blink of an eye. That would have killed me." He took a breath. "I really, really miss you, Kate."

"And?" she coaxed.

Jackson blew out a breath. "And I love you?"

She pressed her lips together to hold back a grin. "Is that a question?"

"It's anything you want it to be," he said in exasperation. "But no, it's not a question. No matter what you feel, I love you." He took a breath. "That's not the easiest phrase for me to say, Kate," he admitted.

"Yes, I know." She looked at him for a long moment. He'd "shown her his." It was time she did the same. "And as for what I feel—" She closed her eyes, seeking courage. Wondering if she was going to regret this. But love *did* take courage. And maybe, just maybe, a prince frog was really a frog prince after all. "I love you."

His arms went around her immediately, but she put her hands against his chest, holding him back. There were more questions she needed to resolve. "Do you really mean it, or are you just saying it because you think that's what I want to hear?"

"Yes. And yes. Yes, I really mean it and yes, I said it because I thought that was what you wanted to hear."

"Otherwise you wouldn't say it?" she questioned.

He feathered his fingers through her hair. He'd *really* missed touching her. "I was raised to believe that actions spoke louder than words."

"It's a toss up," she acknowledged. "Actions are good, but so are words."

He wanted to prove his point. "That guy you were engaged to, did he say he loved you?"

"Yes," she admitted reluctantly. "He did."

"And did he? Did he love you? Did he love you the way you deserved to be loved?" Jackson pressed, then answered his own question. "I don't think so because, if he did, he wouldn't have cheated on you."

Okay, he had a point, but that still didn't mean she didn't want to hear Jackson tell her he loved her. A woman needed words. "Look, maybe—"

"Me," Jackson went on doggedly, "I will never cheat on you. Because it's wrong to cheat on the mother of your children."

Kate held up her hand. "Hold it. How did I go from being the person you couldn't say 'I love you' to to the mother of your children?" she asked.

"Gradually, I hope." His eyes smiled into hers. "I want us to have a couple of years together first before we become a family."

Had he just glossed over a marriage proposal? "Aren't you taking a lot for granted here?"

"Nope, not a thing." Jackson paused to take out a small black velvet box from his pocket. He'd shown it to her mother first, to prove that he was serious before he took her into his confidence and asked for help. Opening the box, he offered the heart-shaped diamond to her. "Katherine Colleen Manetti, will you make me—

and your mother—the two happiest people on the face of the earth?"

"And how can I do that?" Kate found she could hardly squeeze out the words. Her throat had all but closed on her.

"Tell me you'll marry me."

She took a deep breath in an attempt to steady her pulse. "Not bad," she murmured. "Still needs work, but you're getting there."

His eyes held hers. "Does that mean yes?"

She let him put the ring on her finger, then wove her arms around his neck. Tonight, she thought, she was going to sleep like a baby. Eventually.

"What do you think?" she countered.

His arms closed around her. "I think if I don't kiss you, I'm going to explode."

"Can't have—"

His mouth came down on hers and she didn't get a chance to get to the last word. But it was okay. Some things were just understood between two people who loved each other.

* * * * *

Don't miss Marie Ferrarella's next romance,
CAVANAUGH JUDGMENT, *available June 2010*
from Silhouette Romantic Suspense.

Harlequin offers a romance for every mood!
See below for a sneak peek
from our suspense romance line
Silhouette® Romantic Suspense.
Introducing HER HERO IN HIDING by
New York Times *bestselling author Rachel Lee.*

Kay Young returned to woozy consciousness to find that she was lying on a soft sofa beneath a heap of quilts near a cheerfully burning fire. When she tried to move, however, everything hurt, and she groaned.

At once she heard a sound, then a stranger with a hard, harsh face was squatting beside her. "Shh," he said softly. "You're safe here. I promise."

"I have to go," she said weakly, struggling against pain. "He'll find me. He can't find me."

"Easy, lady," he said quietly. "You're hurt. No one's going to find you here."

"He will," she said desperately, terror clutching at her insides. "He always finds me!"

"Easy," he said again. "There's a blizzard outside. No one's getting here tonight, not even the doctor. I know, because I tried."

"Doctor? I don't need a doctor! I've got to get away."

"There's nowhere to go tonight," he said levelly. "And if I thought you could stand, I'd take you to a window and show you."

But even as she tried once more to pull away the quilts, she remembered something else: this man had been gentle when he'd found her beside the road, even when she had kicked and clawed. He hadn't hurt her.

Terror receded just a bit. She looked at him and detected signs of true concern there.

The terror eased another notch and she let her head sag on the pillow. "He always finds me," she whispered.

"Not here. Not tonight. That much I can guarantee."

Will Kay's mysterious rescuer
protect her from her worst fears?
Find out in HER HERO IN HIDING by New York Times *bestselling author Rachel Lee.*
Available June 2010,
only from Silhouette® Romantic Suspense.

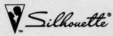

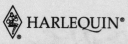

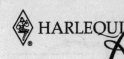

HARLEQUIN® *Romance*®

GIRLS' *Weekend in* VEGAS

Four friends, four dream weddings!

On a girly weekend in Las Vegas, best friends Alex, Molly, Serena and Jayne are supposed to just have fun and forget men, but they end up meeting their perfect matches! Will the love they find in Vegas stay in Vegas?

Find out in this sassy, fun and wildly romantic miniseries all about love and friendship!

═══════════════

Saving Cinderella! by MYRNA MACKENZIE
Available June

Vegas Pregnancy Surprise by SHIRLEY JUMP
Available July

Inconveniently Wed! by JACKIE BRAUN
Available August

Wedding Date with the Best Man
by MELISSA MCCLONE
Available September

www.eHarlequin.com

HARLEQUIN
Ambassadors

Want to share your passion for reading Harlequin® Books?

Become a Harlequin Ambassador!

Harlequin Ambassadors are a group of passionate and well-connected readers who are willing to share their joy of reading Harlequin® books with family and friends.

You'll be sent all the tools you need to spark great conversation, including free books!

All we ask is that you share the romance with your friends and family!

You'll also be invited to have a say in new book ideas and exchange opinions with women just like you!

To see if you qualify* to be a Harlequin Ambassador, please visit
www.HarlequinAmbassadors.com.

*Please note that not everyone who applies to be a Harlequin Ambassador will qualify. For more information please visit www.HarlequinAmbassadors.com.

Thank you for your participation.

BADX9BPA

Love Inspired®

Bestselling author

JILLIAN HART

brings you another heartwarming story
from

the
GRANGER
FAMILY
RANCH

Rancher Justin Granger hasn't seen his high school sweetheart
since she rode out of town with his heart. Now she's back, with
sadness in her eyes, seeking a job as his cook and housekeeper.
He agrees but is determined to avoid her...until he discovers
that her big dream has always been him!

The Rancher's Promise

Available June
wherever books are sold.

Steeple
Hill®

LI87601

REQUEST YOUR FREE BOOKS!

2 FREE NOVELS PLUS 2 FREE GIFTS!

SPECIAL EDITION
Life, Love and Family!

YES! Please send me 2 FREE Silhouette® Special Edition® novels and my 2 FREE gifts (gifts are worth about $10). After receiving them, if I don't wish to receive any more books, I can return the shipping statement marked "cancel." If I don't cancel, I will receive 6 brand-new novels every month and be billed just $4.24 per book in the U.S. or $4.99 per book in Canada. That's a saving of 15% off the cover price! It's quite a bargain! Shipping and handling is just 50¢ per book.* I understand that accepting the 2 free books and gifts places me under no obligation to buy anything. I can always return a shipment and cancel at any time. Even if I never buy another book from Silhouette, the two free books and gifts are mine to keep forever.

235/335 SDN E5RG

Name	(PLEASE PRINT)	
Address		Apt. #
City	State/Prov.	Zip/Postal Code

Signature (if under 18, a parent or guardian must sign)

Mail to the Silhouette Reader Service:
IN U.S.A.: P.O. Box 1867, Buffalo, NY 14240-1867
IN CANADA: P.O. Box 609, Fort Erie, Ontario L2A 5X3

Not valid for current subscribers to Silhouette Special Edition books.

Want to try two free books from another line?
Call 1-800-873-8635 or visit www.morefreebooks.com.

* Terms and prices subject to change without notice. Prices do not include applicable taxes. N.Y. residents add applicable sales tax. Canadian residents will be charged applicable provincial taxes and GST. Offer not valid in Quebec. This offer is limited to one order per household. All orders subject to approval. Credit or debit balances in a customer's account(s) may be offset by any other outstanding balance owed by or to the customer. Please allow 4 to 6 weeks for delivery. Offer available while quantities last.

Your Privacy: Silhouette is committed to protecting your privacy. Our Privacy Policy is available online at www.eHarlequin.com or upon request from the Reader Service. From time to time we make our lists of customers available to reputable third parties who may have a product or service of interest to you. If you would prefer we not share your name and address, please check here. ☐

Help us get it right—We strive for accurate, respectful and relevant communications. To clarify or modify your communication preferences, visit us at www.ReaderService.com/consumerschoice.

SSE10R